# KAHLIL GIBRAN

# Secrets of the Heart

TRANSLATED FROM THE ARABIC
BY ANTHONY RIZCALLAH FERRIS
*and*
EDITED BY MARTIN L. WOLF

**A Citadel Press Book**
**Published by Carol Publishing Group**

First Carol Publishing Group Edition 1992

A Citadel Press Book
Published by Carol Publishing Group
Citadel Press is a registered trademark of Carol Communications, Inc.

Editorial Offices : 600 Madison Avenue, New York, NY  10022
Sales & Distribution Offices:  120 Enterprise Avenue, Secaucus, NJ  07094
In Canada: Canadian Manda Group, P.O. Box 920, Station U, Toronto,
Ontario,  M8Z 5P9, Canada

Queries regarding rights and permissions should be addressed to Carol
Publishing Group, 600 Madison Avenue, New York, NY  10022

Manufactured in the United States of America
ISBN 0-8065-0062-X

Carol Publishing Group books are available at special discounts
for bulk purchases, for sales promotions, fund raising, or
educational purposes.  Special editions can also be created to
specifications. For details contact:  Special Sales Department,
Carol Publishing Group, 120 Enterprise Ave., Secaucus, NJ  07094

25   24   23   22   21   20   19   18   17   16

# Editor's Preface

Pursuing the same fascinating style of his now famous *Tears and Laughter* and *Spirits Rebellious,* Kahlil Gibran conveys a strong and beautiful message in this, another of his earlier works.

The very heart of the mystic East emerges in this volume, and from the outset one feels the tremendous mood, the electrifying boldness, the terrible magnetism of the immortal Gibran.

This ancient wisdom, set forth in the form of a simple yet profound philosophy of life, applies dynamically and with amazing timeliness to present human problems. But for all of his preoccupation with momentous subjects, Gibran is far from the modern school of poetry, and his style inclines to Victorian lyricism when not catapulting toward Dante or Goethe. It is at the same time powerful and tender; frightening and delightful; joyous and funereal; simple and tremendous. However, diametric opposites in substance apparently presented no difficulty in style to this master of simple, effective communication of subtle thought. Gibran's style is incomparable in both poetry and prose, and his prose carries a lyric beauty rich in magnificent simplicity—the simplicity which Gibran continually sought as the identifying characteristic of true beauty in any form.

Yet, in employing the soft phraseology of the Psalms, he nevertheless releases an unrestrained vituperation when execrating the usurpation of human rights by tyrannical church and state officials. It was of little surprise—or importance —to Gibran's multitude of followers that he was exiled from his country and excommunicated from his church in consequence of his fearless, knife-edged attacks. Indicative of his literary artistry, the flowing beauty of his lyrics does not palliate the strength of his indictments, nor does his bitterness invade the exquisite delicacy of his lacy poetry which has an appeal comparable to that of rich music.

Although these atmospheric writings appear to

be autobiographical in nature, they clearly reveal Kahlil Gibran as a prophet of penetrating vision and objective understanding. This seer warns ominously of the grave and unseen dangers yet to befall this world on its stony path of intrigue, maladjustment, and border consciousness. His clarity of perception is not confined to recognition and condemnation alone, but with a sincere constructive purpose motivated by his intense artist's faith in ultimate perfection, he offers strikingly logical methods for curing "the gaping wounds in the side of society." His warnings are neither crusades nor preachments, yet his thoughts are conveyed completely, clearly, powerfully. He muses over the beautiful, not the ugly, and his criticisms are heavily imbued with a gentle melancholy. All, however, are subordinated to his magnificent descriptive powers, abounding with fine metaphorical terseness.

On the ecclesiastical side, he displays a brilliance of spiritual insight and a determination of dedication that persist and probe until they pierce the outer self. His millions of followers in dozens of languages absorb Gibran's writings practically as religious devotions, and his excommunication served to fortify and augment his literary parish. His views of the church are more denunciatory than complimentary, but his love for its teachings and his fury over its methods are sharply defined, and bespeak no ambiguity or paradox in his meaning.

The book burners and clergy lived to rue their acts, and shortly before his death in 1931—perhaps when he was too weak to resist—Gibran submitted to the uninvited overtures of the church to reclaim him after the hasty excommunication. Despite the fact that "The Beloved Master" brought down the unconcealed wrath of religious and state authorities, any apology on his part was of little concern to him, for he had long since reached a spiritual plane far above petty rote, law, and doctrine.

Gibran's doctrine is of kindness, of brotherhood, and of charity, and he requires but few words to transmit great thoughts. On charity he discloses:

*I sing the praise of my home and long to see again my birthplace; but if it refused shelter and food to the needy wayfarer, I would, in my inner voice, convert my praise into eulogy, and my longing into forgetfulness.*

## And again:

*Remember, my brother, that the coin which you drop into the withered hand stretching toward you is the only golden chain that binds your rich heart to the loving heart of God.*

## On brotherhood:

*Love is stronger than death, and death is stronger than life; it is sad that men divide amongst themselves.*

## He adds:

*Humanity is the spirit of the Supreme Being on earth, and humanity is standing amidst unseen ruins, hiding its nakedness behind tattered rags, shedding tears upon hollow cheeks, calling for its children in pitiful voice. But the children are busy singing the anthem; they are busy sharpening the swords and cannot hear the cries of their mothers.*

Small wonder that the present world gives heed to Gibran in its acute difficulty! His thoughts are ageless, and the real, the essential Gibran will live on and grow through the centuries.

He attacks without reservation hypocrisy in any form. Illustrative of his thoughts is the stinging reproach found in "The Crucified," written on Good Friday:

> On this one day of each year, the philosophers leave their dark caves, and the thinkers their cold cells, and the poets their imaginary arbors, and all stand reverently upon that silent mountain, listening to the voice of a young man saying of His tormentors and His killers, "Oh Father, forgive them, for they know not what they are doing."
>
> But as dark silence chokes the voices of light, the philosophers and the thinkers and the poets return to their narrow crevices and shroud their souls with meaningless pages of parchment. The women who busy themselves with the splendour of life will bestir themselves today from their cushions to see the sorrowful woman standing before the Cross, washing with her tears the blood stains from the feet of a Holy Man suspended between heaven and earth; and when their shallow eyes weary of the scene they will depart and soon laugh. The torrent shall sweep away all things not fastened to strength!

*       *       *       *       *

Gibran was young at the time of these writings, but he exhibits a ripe and mature grasp on a subject that has intrigued and baffled man from the beginning—his destiny, and the "why" of his be-

viii

ing. His youth renders all the more remarkable his unquestioned mastery of symbolism and simile, sparkling in profusion throughout "Secrets of the Heart." His sympathetic approach to the prospect of death likewise belongs to the aged, but a knowledge of Gibran's love for tears, which "sear and purify the soul" and his affection for fellow sufferers, offer understanding of his philosophically pleasant contemplations of death.

Generally, Gibran's depth establishes itself at a level of complete lucidity to all who endeavor to find it, and his frequent meanderings into the field of mysticism supplement with spiritual argument the precepts of his earthly discourse. His blending of oriental and occidental philosophy is occasionally disconcerting to the Western mind. One has the feeling that the emotions expressed so plainly were too large for words, and were wrenched from him reluctantly through his soul's compulsion. One cannot fail to recognize in Kahlil Gibran the sincere expression of a passionate urge to improve the lot of suffering, exploited humanity, an impulse that fired his mind and heart from childhood. It is a message, moreover, that emanates from painful knowledge of man's inhumanity to man, drawn from a poignant memory of what his eyes had seen and his ears had heard in his close observance of the perpetual human tragedy.

Gibran drives these teachings forcefully to the heart, and they persist in agitating the heart to complete accord. Like Beethoven's deathless music, of which the composer said, "From the heart it has sprung and to the heart it shall penetrate," this Lebanese Savant, through his rich sincerity, reaches the deepest recesses of our emotional and spiritual awareness.

MARTIN L. WOLF

New York City

1947

# Contents

# The Tempest

# The Tempest

Yusif El Fakhri was thirty years of age when he withdrew himself from society and departed to live in an isolated hermitage in the vicinity of Kedeesha Valley in North Lebanon. The people of the nearby villages heard various tales concerning Yusif; some related that his was a wealthy and noble family, and that he loved a woman who betrayed him and caused him to lead a solitary life, while others said that he was a poet who deserted the clamourous city and retired to that place in order to record his thoughts and compose his inspiration; and many were sure that he was a mystic who was contented with the spiritual world, although most people insisted that he was a madman.

As for myself, I could not draw any conclusion

3

regarding the man, for I knew that there must be a deep secret within his heart whose revelation I would not trust to mere speculation. I had long hoped for the opportunity to meet this strange man. I had endeavoured in devious ways to win his friendship in order to study his reality and learn his story by inquiring as to his purpose in life, but my efforts were in vain. When I met him for the first time, he was walking by the forest of the Holy Cedars of Lebanon, and I greeted him with the finest choice of words, but he returned my greeting by merely shaking his head and striding off.

On another occasion I found him standing in the midst of a small vineyard by a monastery, and again I approached and greeted him, saying, "It is said by the villagers that this monastery was built by a Syriac group in the Fourteenth Century; do you know anything of its history?" He replied coldly, "I do not know who built this monastery, nor do I care to know." And he turned his back to me and added, "Why do you not ask your grandparents, who are older than I, and who know

4

more of the history of these valleys than I do?" Realizing at once my utter failure, I left him.

Thus did two years pass, and the bizarre life of this strange man preyed on my mind and disturbed my dreams.

PART II

One day in Autumn, as I was roaming the hills and knolls adjacent to the hermitage of Yusif El Fakhri, I was suddenly caught in a strong wind and torrent rain, and the tempest cast me here and there like a boat whose rudder has been broken and whose masts have been torn by a gale in a rough sea. I directed my steps with difficulty toward Yusif's place, saying to myself, "This is an opportunity I have long sought, and the tempest will be my excuse for entering, while my wet clothes will serve as good reason for lingering."

I was in a miserable plight when I reached the hermitage, and as I knocked on the door, the man whom I had been longing to see opened it. He was holding in one hand a dying bird whose head had been injured and whose wings had been broken. I greeted him saying, "I beg your forgiveness for this annoying intrusion. The raging tempest trapped me while I was afar from home." He frowned, saying, "There are many caves in this wilderness in which you might have taken refuge." However, he did not close the door, and the beat of my heart quickened in anticipation, for the realization of my great wish was close at hand. He commenced to touch the bird's head gently and with the utmost care and interest, exhibiting a quality important to my heart. I was surprised over the two opponent characteristics I found in that man—mercy and cruelty at the same time. We became aware of the strained silence. He resented my presence, I desired to remain.

It seemed as if he felt my thought, for he looked up and said, "The tempest is clean, and declines to eat soured meat. Why do you seek to escape from it?" And with a touch of humour, I responded, "The tempest may not desire salted or soured things, but she is inclined to chill and tender all things, and undoubtedly she would

6

enjoy consuming me if she grasped me again." His expression was severe when he retorted, "The tempest would have bestowed upon you a great honour, of which you are not worthy, if she had swallowed you." I agreed, "Yes, Sir, I fled the tempest so I might not be awarded an honour which I do not merit." He turned his face from me in an effort to choke his smile, and then motioned toward a wooden bench by the fire-place and invited me to rest and dry my raiment. I could scarcely control my elation.

I thanked him and sat down while he seated himself opposite, on a bench carved of rock. He commenced to dip his finger tips into an earthen-ware jar containing a kind of oil, applying it softly to the bird's head and wings. Without looking up he said, "The strong winds have caused this bird to fall upon the rocks between Life and Death." I replied, rendering comparison, "And the strong winds have sent me, adrift, to your door, in time to prevent having my head injured and my wings broken."

He looked at me seriously and said, "It is my

wish that man would show the bird's instinct, and it is my wish that the tempest would break the people's wings. For man inclines toward fear and cowardice, and as he feels the awakening of the tempest he crawls into the crevices and the caves of the earth and hides himself."

My purpose was to extract the story of his self-imposed exile, and I provoked, "Yes, the birds possess an honour and courage that man does not possess. . . . Man lives in the shadow of laws and customs which he made and fashioned for himself, but the birds live according to the same free Eternal Law which causes the earth to pursue its mighty path about the sun." His eyes and face brightened, as if he had found in me an understanding disciple, and he exclaimed, "Well done! If you place belief in your own words you should leave civilization and its corrupt laws and traditions, and live like the birds in a place empty of all things except the magnificent law of heaven and earth.

"Believing is a fine thing, but placing those beliefs into execution is a test of strength. Many are

8

those who talk like the roar of the sea, but their lives are shallow and stagnant, like the rotting marshes. Many are those who lift their heads above the mountain tops, but their spirits remain dormant in the obscurity of the caverns." He rose trembling from his seat and placed the bird upon a folded cloth by the window.

He placed a bundle of dry sticks upon the fire, saying, "Remove your sandals and warm your feet, for dampness is dangerous to man's health. Dry well your garments, and be comfortable."

Yusif's continued hospitality kept my hopes high. I approached near to the fire, and the steam sifted from my wet robe. While he stood at the door gazing at the grey skies, my mind searched and scurried for the opening wedge into his background. I asked, innocently, "Has it been long since you came to this place?"

Without looking at me, he answered quietly, "I came to this place when the earth was without form, and void; and darkness was upon the face of the deep. And the Spirit of God moved upon the face of the waters."

9

I was aghast at these words! Struggling to gather my shocked and scattered wits, I said to myself, "How fantastic this man is! And how difficult is the path that leads to his reality! But I shall attack cautiously and slowly and patiently, until his reticence turns into communication, and his strangeness into understanding."

### PART III

Night was spreading her black garment upon those valleys, and the tempest was shrieking dizzily and the rain becoming stronger. I began to fancy that the Biblical flood was coming again, to abolish life and wash man's filth from God's earth.

It seemed that the revolution of elements had created in Yusif's heart a tranquility which often comes as a reaction to temperament and converts aloneness into conviviality. He ignited two candles, and then placed before me a jar of wine and a large tray containing bread, cheese, olives, honey, and some dry fruits. Then he sat near me, and after apologizing for the small quantity—but not for the simplicity—of the food, asked me to join him.

We partook of the repast in understanding silence, listening to the wailing of the wind and the crying of the rain, and at the same time I was contemplating his face and trying to dig out his secrets, meditating the possible motive underlying his unusual existence. Having finished, he took a copper kettle from the fire and poured pure, aromatic coffee into two cups; then he opened a small box and offered me a cigarette, addressing me as "Brother." I took one while drinking my coffee, not believing what my eyes were seeing. He looked at me smilingly, and after he had inhaled deeply of his cigarette and sipped some coffee, he said, "Undoubtedly you are thinking upon the existence here of wine and tobacco and coffee, and you may also be wondering over my food and comforts. Your curiosity is justified in all respects, for you are one of the many who believe that in being away from the people, one is absent from life, and must abstain from all its enjoyment." Quickly I agreed, "Yes, it is related by the wise men that he who deserts the world for the purpose of worshipping God alone will leave behind all the enjoyment and plenty of life, contenting himself with the simple products of God alone, and existing on plants and water."

After a pause, heavy with thought, he mused, "I could have worshipped God while living among His creatures, for worship does not require solitude. I did not leave the people in order to see God, for I had always seen Him at the home of my father and mother. I deserted the people because their natures were in conflict with mine, and their dreams did not agree with my dreams. . . . I left man because I found that the wheel of my soul was turning one way and grinding harshly against the wheels of other souls which were turning in the opposite direction. I left civilization because I found it to be an old and corrupt tree, strong and terrible, whose roots are locked into the obscurity of the earth and whose branches are reaching beyond the cloud; but its blossoms are of greed and evil and crime, and its fruit is of woe and misery and fear. Crusaders have undertaken to blend good into it and change its nature, but they could not succeed. They died disappointed, persecuted and torn."

Yusif leaned toward the side of the fireplace as if awaiting the impression of his words upon my heart. I thought it best to remain a listener, and he continued, "No, I did not seek solitude to pray and lead a hermit's life . . . for prayer, which is the song of the heart, will reach the ears of God even when mingled with the shout and cry of thousands of voices. To live the life of a recluse is to torture the body and soul and deaden the inclinations, a kind of existence which is repugnant to me, for God has erected the bodies as temples for the spirits, and it is our mission to deserve and maintain the trust reposed in us by God.

"No, my brother, I did not seek solitude for religious purposes, but solely to avoid the people and their laws, their teachings and their traditions, their ideas and their clamour and their wailing.

"I sought solitude in order to keep from seeing the faces of men who sell themselves and buy with the same price that which is lower than they are, spiritually and materially.

"I sought solitude in order that I might not encounter the women who walk proudly, with one thousand smiles upon their lips, while in the depths of their thousands of hearts there is but one purpose.

"I sought solitude in order to conceal myself from those self-satisfied individuals who see the spectre of knowledge in their dreams and believe that they have attained their goal.

"I fled from society to avoid those who see but the phantom of truth in their awakening, and shout to the world that they have acquired completely the essence of truth.

"I deserted the world and sought solitude because I became tired of rendering courtesy to those multitudes who believe that humility is a sort of weakness, and mercy a kind of cowardice, and snobbery a form of strength.

"I sought solitude because my soul wearied of

14

association with those who believe sincerely that the sun and moon and stars do not rise save from their coffers, and do not set except in their gardens.

"I ran from the office-seekers who shatter the earthly fate of the people while throwing into their eyes the golden dust and filling their ears with sounds of meaningless talk.

"I departed from the ministers who do not live according to their sermons, and who demand of the people that which they do not solicit of themselves.

"I sought solitude because I never obtained kindness from a human unless I paid the full price with my heart.

"I sought solitude because I loathe that great and terrible institution which the people call civilization—that symmetrical monstrosity erected upon the perpetual misery of human kinds.

"I sought solitude for in it there is a full life for the spirit and for the heart and for the body. I found the endless prairies where the light of the sun rests, and where the flowers breathe their fragrance into space, and where the streams sing their way to the sea. I discovered the mountains where I found the fresh awakening of Spring, and the colourful longing of Summer, and the rich songs of Autumn, and the beautiful mystery of Winter. I came to this far corner of God's domain for I hungered to learn the secrets of the Universe, and approach close to the throne of God."

\*　　　\*　　　\*　　　\*　　　\*

Yusif breathed deeply, as if he had been relieved of a heavy burden. His eyes shone with strange and magical rays, and upon his radiant face appeared the signs of pride, will, and contentment.

A few minutes passed, and I was gazing placidly at him, and pondering the unveiling of what had been hidden from me; then I addressed him, saying, "You are undoubtedly correct in most of the things you have said, but through your diagnosis of the social ailment, you prove at the same time that you are a good doctor. I believe that the sick society is in dire need of such a physician, who should cure it or kill it. This distressed world begs your attention. Is it just or merciful to withdraw yourself from the ailing patient and deny him your benefit?"

He stared at me thoughtfully, and then said with futility, "Since the beginning of the world, the doctors have been trying to save the people from their disorders; some used knives, while others used potions, but pestilence spread hopelessly. It is my wish that the patient would content himself with remaining in his filthy bed, meditating his long-continued sores; but instead, he stretches his hands from under the robe and clutches at the neck of each who comes to visit him, choking him to death. What irony it is! The evil patient kills the doctor, and then closes his eyes and says within himself, 'He was a great physician.' No, Brother, no one on earth can benefit humanity. The sower, however wise and expert he may be, cannot cause the field to sprout in Winter."

And I argued, "The people's Winter will pass away, and then comes the beautiful Spring, and the flowers must surely bloom in the fields, and the brooks will again leap in the valleys."

He frowned, and said bitterly, "Alas! Has God divided man's life—which is the whole creation —into seasons like those of the year? Will any tribe of human beings, living now in God's truth and spirit, desire to re-appear on the face of this earth? Will ever the time come when man settles and abides at the right arm of Life, rejoicing with the brilliant light of day and the peaceful silence of night? Can that dream become reality? Can it materialize after the earth has been covered with human flesh and drenched with man's blood?"

And Yusif stood and raised his hand toward the sky, as if pointing at a different world, and he continued, "This is naught but a vain dream for the world, but I am finding its accomplishment for myself, and what I am discovering here occupies every space in my heart and in the valleys and in the mountains." He now raised his intense voice, "What I really know to be true is the crying of my inner self. I am here living, and in the depths of my existence there is a thirst and hunger, and I find joy in partaking of the bread and wine of Life from the vases which I make and fashion by my own hands. For this reason I abandoned the boards of the people and came to this place, and I shall remain here until the Ending!"

He continued walking back and forth across the room in agitation while I was pondering his sayings and meditating the description of society's gaping wounds. I ventured again a tactful criticism. "I hold the utmost regard for your opinion and intentions, and I envy and respect your solitude and aloneness, but I know that this miserable nation has sustained a great loss in your expatriation, for she is in need of an understanding healer to help her through her difficulties and awaken her spirit."

He shook his head slowly and said, "This nation is like all the nations. And the people are made of the same element and do not vary except in their exterior appearance, which is of no consequence. The misery of our Oriental nations is the misery of the world, and what you call civilization in the West is naught but another spectre of the many phantoms of tragic deception.

"Hypocrisy will always remain, even if her finger tips are coloured and polished; and Deceit will never change even if her touch becomes soft and delicate; and Falsehood will never turn into Truth even if you dress her with silken robes and place her in the palace; and Greed will not become Contentment; nor will Crime become Virtue. And Eternal Slavery to teachings, to customs, and to history will remain Slavery even if she paints her face and disguises her voice. Slavery will remain Slavery in all her horrible form, even if she calls herself Liberty.

"No, my brother, the West is not higher than the East, nor is the West lower than the East, and the difference that stands between the two is not greater than the difference between the tiger and the lion. There is a just and perfect law that I have found behind the exterior of society, which equalizes misery, prosperity, and ignorance; it does not prefer one nation to another, nor does it oppress one tribe in order to enrich another."

20

I exclaimed, "Then civilization is vanity, and all in it is vanity!" He quickly responded, "Yes, civilization is vanity and all in it is vanity. . . . Inventions and discoveries are but amusement and comfort for the body when it is tired and weary. The conquest of distance and the victory over the seas are but false fruit which do not satisfy the soul, nor nourish the heart, neither lift the spirit, for they are afar from nature. And those structures and theories which man calls knowledge and art are naught except shackles and golden chains which man drags, and he rejoices with their glittering reflections and ringing sounds. They are strong cages whose bars man commenced fabricating ages ago, unaware that he was building from the inside, and that he would soon become his own prisoner to eternity. Yes, vain are the deeds of man, and vain are his purposes, and all is vanity upon this earth." He paused, then slowly added, "And among all vanities of life, there is only one thing that the spirit loves and craves. One thing dazzling and alone."

"What is it?" I inquired with quivering voice.

He looked at me for a long minute and then closed his eyes. He placed his hands on his chest, while his face brightened, and with a serene and sincere voice he said, "It is an awakening in the spirit; it is an awakening in the inner depths of the heart; it is an overwhelming and magnificent power that descends suddenly upon man's conscience and opens his eyes, whereupon he sees Life amid a dizzying shower of brilliant music, surrounded by a circle of great light, with man standing as a pillar of beauty between the earth and the firmament. It is a flame that suddenly rages within the spirit and sears and purifies the heart, ascending above the earth and hovering in the spacious sky. It is a kindness that envelops the individual's heart whereby he would bewilder and disapprove all who opposed it, and revolt against those who refuse to understand its great meaning. It is a secret hand which removed the veil from my eyes while i was a member of society amidst my family, my friends and my countrymen.

"Many times I wondered, and spoke to myself, saying, 'What is this Universe, and why am I different from those people who are looking at me, and how do I know them, and where did I meet them, and why am I living among them? Am I a stranger among them, or is it they who are strange to this earth, built by Life who entrusted me with the keys?' "

He suddenly became silent, as if remembering something he had seen long before, refusing to reveal it. Then he stretched his arms forward and whispered, "That is what happened to me four years ago, when I left the world and came to this void place to live in the awakeness of life and enjoy kind thoughts and beautiful silence."

He walked toward the door, looking at the depths of the darkness as if preparing to address the tempest. But he spoke in a vibrating voice, saying, "It is an awakening within the spirit; he who knows it, is unable to reveal it by words; and he who knows it not, will never think upon the compelling and beautiful mystery of existence."

## PART IV

An hour had passed and Yusif El Fakhri was striding about the room, stopping at random and gazing at the tremendous grey skies. I remained silent, reflecting upon the strange unison of joy and sorrow in his solitary life.

Later in the night he approached me and stared long into my face, as if wanting to commit to memory the picture of the man to whom he had disclosed the piercing secrets of his life. My mind was heavy with turmoil, my eyes with mist. He said quietly, "I am going now to walk through the night with the tempest, to feel the closeness of Nature's expression; it is a practise that I enjoy greatly in Autumn and Winter. Here is the wine, and there is the tobacco; please accept my home as your own for the night."

He wrapped himself in a black robe and added smilingly, "I beg you to fasten the door against the intruding humans when you leave in the morning, for I plan to spend the day in the forest of the Holy Cedars." Then he walked toward the

24

door, carrying a long walking staff and he concluded, "If the tempest surprises you again while you are in this vicinity, do not hesitate to take refuge in this hermitage. . . . I hope you will teach yourself to love, and not to fear, the tempest. . . . Good night, my brother."

He opened the door and walked out with his head high, into the dark. I stood at the door to see which course he had taken, but he had disappeared from view. For a few minutes I heard the fall of his feet upon the broken stones of the valley.

### PART V

Morning came, after a night of deep thought, and the tempest had passed away, while the sky was clear and the mountains and the plains were reveling in the sun's warm rays. On my way back to the city I felt that spiritual awakening of which Yusif El Fakhri had spoken, and it was raging throughout every fibre of my being. I felt that my shivering must be visible. And when I calmed, all about me was beauty and perfection.

As soon as I reached the noisome people and heard their voices and saw their deeds, I stopped and said within myself, "Yes, the spiritual awakening is the most essential thing in man's life, and it is the sole purpose of being. Is not civilization, in all its tragic forms, a supreme motive for spiritual awakening? Then how can we deny existing matter, while its very existence is unwavering proof of its conformability into the intended fitness? The present civilization may possess a vanishing purpose, but the eternal law has offered to that purpose a ladder whose steps can lead to a free substance."

*　　*　　*　　*　　*

I never saw Yusif El Fakhri again, for through my endeavours to attend the ills of civilization, Life had expelled me from North Lebanon in late Autumn of that same year, and I was required to live in exile in a distant country whose tempests are domestic. And leading a hermit's life in that country is a sort of glorious madness, for its society, too, is ailing.

*Slavery*

# Slavery

THE PEOPLE are the slaves of Life, and it is slavery which fills their days with misery and distress, and floods their nights with tears and anguish.

Seven thousand years have passed since the day of my first birth, and since that day I have been witnessing the slaves of Life, dragging their heavy shackles.

I have roamed the East and West of the earth and wandered in the Light and in the Shadow of Life. I have seen the processions of civilization moving from light into darkness, and each was dragged down to hell by humiliated souls bent under the yoke of slavery. The strong is fettered and subdued, and the faithful is on his knees worshipping before the idols. I have followed man from Babylon to Cairo, and from Ain Dour to Baghdad, and observed the marks of his chains upon the sand. I heard the sad echoes of the fickle ages repeated by the eternal prairies and valleys.

I visited the temples and altars and entered the palaces, and sat before the thrones. And I saw the apprentice slaving for the artisan, and the artisan slaving for the employer, and the employer slaving for the soldier, and the soldier slaving for the governor, and the governor slaving for the king, and the king slaving for the priest, and the priest slaving for the idol. . . . And the idol is naught but earth fashioned by Satan and erected upon a knoll of skulls.

I entered the mansions of the rich and visited the huts of the poor. I found the infant nursing the milk of slavery from his mother's bosom, and the children learning submission with the alphabet.

The maidens wear garments of restriction and passivity, and the wives retire with tears upon beds of obedience and legal compliance.

I accompanied the ages from the banks of the Kange to the shores of Euphrates; from the mouth of the Nile to the plains of Assyria; from the arenas of Athens to the churches of Rome; from the slums of Constantinople to the palaces of Alexandria. . . . Yet I saw slavery moving over all, in a glorious and majestic procession of ignorance. I saw the people sacrificing the youths and maidens at the feet of the idol, calling her the God; pouring wine and perfume upon her feet, and calling her the Queen; burning incense before her image, and calling her the Prophet; kneeling and worshipping before her, and calling her the Law; fighting and dying for her, and calling her Patriotism; submitting to her will, and calling her the Shadow of God on earth; destroying and demolishing homes and institutions for her sake, and calling her Fraternity; struggling and stealing and working for her, and calling her Fortune and Happiness; killing for her, and calling her Equality.

She possesses various names, but one reality. She has many appearances, but is made of one element. In truth, she is an everlasting ailment bequeathed by each generation unto its successor.

\*　　\*　　\*　　\*　　\*

I found the blind slavery, which ties the people's present with their parents' past, and urges them to yield to their traditions and customs, placing ancient spirits in the new bodies.

I found the mute slavery, which binds the life of a man to a wife whom he abhors, and places the woman's body in the bed of a hated husband, deadening both lives spiritually.

I found the deaf slavery, which stifles the soul and the heart, rendering man but an empty echo of a voice, and a pitiful shadow of a body.

I found the lame slavery, which places man's neck under the domination of the tyrant and submits strong bodies and weak minds to the sons of Greed for use as instruments to their power.

I found the ugly slavery, which descends with the infants' spirits from the spacious firmament into the home of Misery, where Need lives by Ignorance, and Humiliation resides beside Despair. And the children grow as miserables, and live as criminals, and die as despised and rejected non-existents.

I found the subtle slavery, which entitles things

with other than their names—calling slyness an intelligence, and emptiness a knowledge, and weakness a tenderness, and cowardice a strong refusal.

I found the twisted slavery, which causes the tongues of the weak to move with fear, and speak outside of their feelings, and they feign to be meditating their plight, but they become as empty sacks, which even a child can fold or hang.

I found the bent slavery, which prevails upon one nation to comply with the laws and rules of another nation, and the bending is greater with each day.

I found the perpetual slavery, which crowns the sons of monarchs as kings, and offers no regard to merit.

I found the black slavery, which brands with shame and disgrace forever the innocent sons of the criminals.

Contemplating slavery, it is found to possess the vicious powers of continuation and contagion.

\*     \*     \*     \*     \*

When I grew tired of following the dissolute ages, and wearied of beholding the processions of stoned people, I walked lonely in the Valley of the Shadow of Life, where the past attempts to conceal itself in guilt, and the soul of the future folds and rests itself too long. There, at the edge of Blood and Tears River, which crawled like a poisonous viper and twisted like a criminal's dreams, I listened to the frightened whisper of the ghosts of slaves, and gazed at nothingness.

When midnight came and the spirits emerged from hidden places, I saw a cadaverous, dying spectre fall to her knees, gazing at the moon. I approached her, asking, "What is your name?"

"My name is Liberty," replied this ghastly shadow of a corpse.

And I inquired, "Where are your children?"

And Liberty, tearful and weak, gasped, "One died crucified, another died mad, and the third one is not yet born."

She limped away and spoke further, but the mist in my eyes and cries of my heart prevented sight or hearing.

34

*Satan*

# Satan

THE PEOPLE looked upon Father Samaan as their guide in the field of spiritual and theological matters, for he was an authority and a source of deep information on venial and mortal sins, well versed in the secrets of Paradise, Hell, and Purgatory.

Father Samaan's mission in North Lebanon was to travel from one village to another, preaching and curing the people from the spiritual disease of sin, and saving them from the horrible trap of Satan. The Reverend Father waged constant war with Satan. The fellahin honoured and respected this clergyman, and were always anxious to buy his advice or prayers with pieces of gold and silver; and at every harvest they would present him with the finest fruits of their fields.

One evening in Autumn, as Father Samaan walked his way toward a solitary village, crossing those valleys and hills, he heard a painful cry emerging from a ditch at the side of the road. He stopped and looked in the direction of the voice, and saw an unclothed man lying on the ground. Streams of blood oozed from deep wounds in his head and chest. He was moaning pitifully for aid, saying, "Save me, help me. Have mercy on me, I am dying." Father Samaan looked with perplexity at the sufferer, and said within himself, "This man must be a thief. . . . He probably tried to rob the wayfarers and failed. Some one has wounded him, and I fear that should he die I may be accused of having taken his life."

Having thus pondered the situation, he resumed his journey, whereupon the dying man stopped him, calling out, "Do not leave me! I am dying!" Then the Father meditated again, and his face became pale as he realized he was refusing to help. His lips quivered, but he spoke to himself, saying, "He must surely be one of the madmen wandering in the wilderness. The sight of his wounds brings fear into my heart; what shall I do? Surely a spiritual doctor is not capable of treating flesh-wounded bodies." Father Samaan walked ahead a few paces when the near-corpse uttered a painful plaint that melted the heart of the rock and he gasped, "Come close to me! Come, for we have been friends a long time. . . . You are Father Samaan, the Good Shepherd, and I am not a thief nor a madman. . . . Come close, and do not let me die in this deserted place. Come, and I will tell you who I am."

Father Samaan came close to the man, knelt, and stared at him; but he saw a strange face with contrasting features; he saw intelligence with slyness, ugliness with beauty, and wickedness with softness. He withdrew to his feet sharply, and exclaimed, "Who are you?"

With a fainting voice, the dying man said, "Fear me not, Father, for we have been strong friends for long. Help me to stand, and take me to the nearby streamlet and cleanse my wounds with your linens." And the Father inquired, "Tell me who you are, for I do not know you, nor even remember having seen you."

And the man replied with an agonizing voice,

"You know my identity! You have seen me one thousand times and you speak of me each day. . . . I am dearer to you than your own life." And the Father reprimanded, "You are a lying imposter! A dying man should tell the truth. . . . I have never seen your evil face in my entire life. Tell me who you are, or I will suffer you to die, soaked in your own escaping life." And the wounded man moved slowly and looked into the clergyman's eyes, and upon his lips appeared a mystic smile; and in a quiet, deep and smooth voice he said, "I am Satan."

Upon hearing the fearful word, Father Samaan uttered a terrible cry that shook the far corners of the valley; then he stared, and realized that the dying man's body, with its grotesque distortions, coincided with the likeness of Satan in a religious picture hanging on the wall of the village church. He trembled and cried out, saying, "God has shown me your hellish image and justly caused me to hate you; cursed be you forevermore! The mangled lamb must be destroyed by the shepherd lest he will infect the other lambs!"

40

Satan answered, "Be not in haste, Father, and lose not this fleeting time in empty talk. . . . Come and close my wounds quickly, before Life departs from my body." And the clergyman retorted, "The hands which offer a daily sacrifice to God shall not touch a body made of the secretion of Hell. . . . You must die accursed by the tongues of the Ages, and the lips of Humanity, for you are the enemy of Humanity, and it is your avowed purpose to destroy all virtue."

Satan moved in anguish, raising himself upon one elbow, and responded, "You know not what you are saying, nor understand the crime you are committing upon yourself. Give heed, for I will relate my story. Today I walked alone in this solitary valley. When I reached this place, a group of angels descended to attack, and struck me severely; had it not been for one of them, who carried a blazing sword with two sharp edges, I would have driven them off, but I had no power against the brilliant sword." And Satan ceased talking for a moment, as he pressed a shaking hand upon a deep wound in his side. Then he continued, "The armed angel—I believe he was Michael—was an expert gladiator. Had I not thrown myself to the friendly ground and feigned to have been slain, he would have torn me into brutal death."

With voice of triumph, and casting his eyes heavenward, the Father offered, "Blessed be Michael's name, who has saved Humanity from this vicious enemy."

And Satan protested, "My disdain for Humanity is not greater than your hatred for yourself. . . . You are blessing Michael who never has come to your rescue. . . . You are cursing me in the hour of my defeat, even though I was, and still am, the source of your tranquility and happiness. . . . You deny me your blessing, and extend not your kindness, but you live and prosper in the shadow of my being. . . . You have adopted for my existence an excuse and weapon for your career, and you employ my name in justification for your deeds. Has not my past caused you to be in need of my present and future? Have you reached your goal in amassing the required wealth? Have you found it impossible to extract more gold and silver from your followers, using my kingdom as a threat?

"Do you not realize that you will starve to death if I were to die? What would you do tomorrow if you allowed me to die today? What vocation would you pursue if my name disappeared? For decades you have been roaming these villages and warning the people against falling into my hands. They have bought your advice with their poor denars and with the products of their land. What would they buy from you tomorrow, if they discovered that their wicked enemy no longer existed? Your occupation would die with me, for the people would be safe from sin. As a clergyman, do you not realize that Satan's existence alone has created his enemy, the church? That ancient conflict is the secret hand which removes the gold and silver from the faithful's pocket and deposits it forever into the pouch of the preacher and missionary. How can you permit me to die here, when you know it will surely cause you to

43

lose your prestige, your church, your home, and
your livelihood?"

*   *   *   *   *

Satan became silent for a moment and his humility was now converted into a confident inde-
pendence, and he continued, "Father, you are
proud, but ignorant. I will disclose to you the
history of belief, and in it you will find the truth
which joins both of our beings, and ties my existence with your very conscience.

"In the first hour of the beginning of time, man
stood before the face of the sun and stretched forth
his arms and cried for the first time, saying, 'Behind the sky there is a great and loving and benev-
olent God.' Then man turned his back to the
great circle of light and saw his shadow upon
the earth, and he hailed, 'In the depths of the
earth there is a dark devil who loves wickedness.'

"And the man walked toward his cave, whispering to himself, 'I am between two compelling
forces, one in whom I must take refuge, and the

other against whom I must struggle.' And the ages marched in procession while man existed between two powers, one that he blessed because it exalted him, and one that he cursed because it frightened him. But he never perceived the meaning of a blessing or of a curse; he was between the two, like a tree between Summer, when it blooms, and Winter, when it shivers.

"When man saw the dawn of civilization, which is human understanding, the family as a unit came into being. Then came the tribes, whereupon labour was divided according to ability and inclination; one clan cultivated the land, another built shelters, others wove raiment or hunted food. Subsequently divination made its appearance upon the earth, and this was the first career adopted by man which possessed no essential urge or necessity."

Satan ceased talking for a moment. Then he laughed and his mirth shook the empty valley, but his laughter reminded him of his wounds, and he placed his hand on his side, suffering with pain. He steadied himself and continued, "Divination appeared and grew on earth in strange fashion.

"There was a man in the first tribe called La Wiss. I know not the origin of his name. He was an intelligent creature, but extremely indolent and he detested work in the cultivation of land, construction of shelters, grazing of cattle or any pursuit requiring body movement or exertion. And since food, during that era, could not be obtained except by arduous toil, La Wiss slept many nights with an empty stomach.

"One Summer night, as the members of that clan were gathered around the hut of their Chief, talking of the outcome of their day and waiting for their slumber time, a man suddenly leaped to his feet, pointed toward the moon, and cried out, saying, 'Look at the Night God! His face is dark, and his beauty has vanished, and he has turned into a black stone hanging in the dome of the sky!' The multitude gazed at the moon, shouted in awe, and shook with fear, as if the hands of darkness had clutched their hearts, for they saw the Night God slowly turning into a dark ball which changed the bright countenance of the earth and caused the hills and valleys before their eyes to disappear behind a black veil.

"At that moment, La Wiss, who had seen an eclipse before, and understood its simple cause, stepped forward to make much of this opportunity. He stood in the midst of the throng, lifted his hands to the sky, and in a strong voice he addressed them, saying, 'Kneel and pray, for the Evil God of Obscurity is locked in struggle with the Illuminating Night God; if the Evil God conquers him, we will all perish, but if the Night God triumphs over him, we will remain alive. . . . Pray now and worship. . . . Cover your faces with earth. . . . Close your eyes, and lift not your heads toward the sky, for he who witnesses the two gods wrestling will lose his sight and mind, and will remain blind and insane all his life! Bend your heads low, and with all your hearts urge the Night God against his enemy, who is our mortal enemy!'

"Thus did La Wiss continue talking, using many cryptic words of his own fabrication which they had never heard. After this crafty deception, as the moon returned to its previous glory, La Wiss raised his voice louder than before and said impressively, 'Rise now, and look at the Night God who has triumphed over his evil enemy. He is resuming his journey among the stars. Let it be known that through your prayers you have helped him to overcome the Devil of Darkness. He is well pleased now, and brighter than ever.'

"The multitude rose and gazed at the moon that was shining in full beam. Their fear became tranquility, and their confusion was now joy. They commenced dancing and singing and striking with their thick sticks upon sheets of iron, filling the valleys with their clamour and shouting.

"That night, the Chief of the tribe called La Wiss and spoke to him, saying, 'You have done something that no man has ever done. . . . You have demonstrated knowledge of a hidden secret that no other among us understands. Reflecting the will of my people, you are to be the highest ranking member, after me, in the tribe. I am the strongest man, and you are the wisest and most learned person. . . . You are the medium between our people and the gods, whose desires and deeds you are to interpret, and you will teach us those things necessary to gain their blessings and love.'

"And La Wiss slyly assured, 'Everything the Human God reveals to me in my divine dreams will be conveyed to you in awakeness, and you may be confident that I will act directly between you and him.' The chief was assured, and gave La Wiss two horses, seven calves, seventy sheep and seventy lambs; and he spoke to him, saying, 'The men of the tribe shall build for you a strong house, and will give you at the end of each harvest season a part of the crop of the land so you may live as an honourable and respected Master.'

"La Wiss rose and started to leave, but the Chief stopped him, saying, 'Who and what is the one whom you call the Human God? Who is this daring God who wrestles with the glorious Night God? We have never pondered him before.' La Wiss rubbed his forehead and answered him, saying, 'My Honourable Master, in the olden time, before the creation of man, all the Gods were living peacefully together in an upper world behind the vastness of the stars. The God of Gods was their father, and knew what they did not know, and did what they were unable to do. He kept for himself the divine secrets that existed beyond the eternal laws. During the seventh epoch of the twelfth age, the spirit of Bahtaar, who hated the great God, revolted and stood before his father, and said, 'Why do you keep for yourself the power of great authority upon all creatures, hiding away from us the secrets and laws of the Universe? Are we not your children who believe in you and share with you the great understanding and the perpetual being?'

"The God of Gods became enraged and said, 'I shall preserve for myself the primary power and the great authority and the essential secrets, for I am the beginning and the end.'

"And Bahtaar answered him saying, 'Unless you share with me your might and power, I and my children and my children's children will revolt against you!' At that moment, the God of Gods stood upon his throne in the deep heavens, and drew forth a sword, and grasped the Sun as a shield; and with a voice that shook all corners of eternity he shouted out, saying, 'Descend, you evil rebel, to the dismal lower world where darkness and misery exist! There you shall remain in exile, wandering until the Sun turns into ashes and the stars into dispersed particles!' In that hour, Bahtaar descended from the upper world into the lower world, where all the evil spirits dwelt. Thereupon, he swore by the secret of Life that he would fight his father and brothers by trapping every soul who loved them.'

"As the Chief listened, his forehead wrinkled and his face turned pale. He ventured, 'Then the name of the Evil God is Bahtaar?' And La Wiss responded, 'His name was Bahtaar when he was in the upper world, but when he entered into the lower world, he adopted successively the names Baalzaboul, Satanail, Balial, Zamiel, Ahriman, Mara, Abdon, Devil, and finally Satan, which is the most famous.'

"The Chief repeated the word 'Satan' many times with a quivering voice that sounded like the rustling of the dry branches at the passing of the wind; then he said, 'Why does Satan hate man as much as he hates the gods?'

"And La Wiss responded quickly, 'He hates man because man is a descendant of Satan's brothers and sisters.' The Chief exclaimed, 'Then Satan is the cousin of man!' In a voice mingled with confusion and annoyance, he retorted, 'Yes, Master, but he is their great enemy who fills their days with misery and their nights with horrible dreams. He is the power who directs the tempest toward their hovels, and brings famine upon their plantation, and disease upon them and their animals. He is an evil and powerful god; he is wicked, and he rejoices when we are in sorrow, and he mourns when we are joyous. We must, through my knowledge, examine him thoroughly, in order to avoid his evil; we must study his character, so we will not step upon his trap-laden path.'

"The Chief leaned his head upon his thick stick and whispered, saying, 'I have learned now the inner secret of that strange power who directs the tempest toward our homes and brings the pestilence upon us and our cattle. The people shall learn all that I have comprehended now, and La Wiss will be blessed, honoured and glorified for revealing to them the mystery of their powerful enemy, and directing them away from the road of evil.'

"And La Wiss left the Chief of the tribe and went to his retiring place, happy over his ingenuity, and intoxicated with the wine of his pleasure and fancy. For the first time, the Chief and all of the tribe, except La Wiss, spent the night slumbering in beds surrounded by horrible ghosts, fearful spectres, and disturbing dreams."

\*      \*      \*      \*      \*

Satan ceased talking for a moment, while Father Samaan stared at him as one bewildered, and upon the Father's lips appeared the sickly laughter of Death. Then Satan continued, "Thus divination came to this earth, and thus was my existence the cause for its appearance. La Wiss was the first who adopted my cruelty as a vocation. After the death of La Wiss, this occupation circulated through his children and prospered until it became a perfect and divine profession, pursued by those whose minds are ripe with knowledge, and whose souls are noble, and whose hearts are pure, and whose fancy is vast.

"In Babylon, the people bowed seven times in worshipping before a priest who fought me with his chantings. . . . In Nineveh, they looked upon a man, who claimed to have known my inner secrets, as a golden link between God and man. . . . In Tibet, they called the person who wrestled with me The Son of the Sun and Moon. . . . In Byblus, Ephesus and Antioch, they offered their children's lives in sacrifice to my opponents. . . . In Jerusalem and Rome, they placed their lives in the hands of those who claimed they hated me and fought me with all their might.

"In every city under the sun my name was the axis of the educational circle of religion, arts, and philosophy. Had it not been for me, no temples would have been built, no towers or palaces would have been erected. I am the courage that creates resolution in man. . . . I am the source that provokes originality of thought. . . . I am the hand that moves man's hands. . . .I am Satan everlasting. I am Satan whom the people fight in order to keep themselves alive. If they cease struggling against me, slothfulness will deaden their minds and hearts and souls, in accordance with the weird penalties of their tremendous myth.

"I am the enraged and mute tempest who agitates the minds of man and the hearts of women. And in fear of me, they will travel to places of worship to condemn me, or to places of vice to make me happy by surrendering to my will. The monk who prays in the silence of the night to keep me away from his bed is like the prostitute who invites me to her chamber. I am Satan everlasting and eternal.

"I am the builder of convents and monasteries upon the foundation of fear. I build wine shops and wicked houses upon the foundations of lust and self-gratification. If I cease to exist, fear and enjoyment will be abolished from the world, and through their disappearance, desires and hopes will cease to exist in the human heart. Life will become empty and cold, like a harp with broken strings. I am Satan everlasting.

"I am the inspiration for Falsehood, Slander, Treachery, Deceit and Mockery, and if these elements were to be removed from this world, human society would become like a deserted field in which naught would thrive but thorns of virtue. I am Satan everlasting.

"I am the father and mother of sin, and if sin were to vanish, the fighters of sin would vanish with it, along with their families and structures.

"I am the heart of all evil. Would you wish for human motion to stop through cessation of my heartbeats? Would you accept the result after destroying the cause? I am the cause! Would you allow me to die in this deserted wilderness? Do you desire to sever the bond that exists between you and me? Answer me, clergyman!"

And Satan stretched his arms and bent his head forward and gasped deeply; his face turned to gray and he resembled one of those Egyptian statues laid waste by the Ages at the side of the Nile. Then he fixed his glittering eyes upon Father Samaan's face, and said, in a faltering voice, "I am tired and weak. I did wrong by using my waning strength to speak on things you already knew. Now you may do as you please. . . . You may carry me to your home and treat my wounds, or leave me in this place to die."

Father Samaan quivered and rubbed his hands nervously, and with apology in his voice he said, "I know now what I had not known an hour ago. Forgive my ignorance. I know that your existence in this world creates temptation, and temptation is a measurement by which God adjudges the value of human souls. It is a scale which Almighty God uses to weigh the spirits. I am certain that if you die, temptation will die, and with its passing, death will destroy the ideal power which elevates and alerts man.

"You must live, for if you die and the people know it, their fear of hell will vanish and they will cease worshipping, for naught would be sin. You must live, for in your life is the salvation of humanity from vice and sin.

"As to myself, I shall sacrifice my hatred for you on the altar of my love for man."

Satan uttered a laugh that rocked the ground, and he said, "What an intelligent person you are, Father! And what wonderful knowledge you possess in theological facts! You have found, through the power of your knowledge, a purpose for my existence which I had never understood, and now we realize our need for each other.

"Come close to me, my brother; darkness is submerging the plains, and half of my blood has escaped upon the sand of this valley, and naught remains of me but the remnants of a broken body which Death shall soon buy unless you render aid." Father Samaan rolled the sleeves of his robe and approached, and lifted Satan to his back and walked toward his home.

*　　*　　*　　*　　*

In the midst of those valleys, engulfed with silence and embellished with the veil of darkness,

Father Samaan walked toward the village with his back bent under his heavy burden. His black raiment and long beard were spattered with blood streaming from above him, but he struggled forward, his lips moving in fervent prayer for the life of the dying Satan.

# The Mermaids

# The Mermaids

In the depths of the sea, surrounding the nearby islands where the sun rises, there is a profoundness. And there, where the pearl exists in abundance, lay a corpse of a youth encircled by sea maidens of long golden hair; they stared upon him with their deep blue eyes, conversing among themselves with musical voices. And the conversation, heard by the depths and conveyed to the shore by the waves, was brought to me by the frolicsome breeze.

One of them said, "This is a human who entered into our world yesterday, while our sea was raging."

And the second one said, "The sea was not raging. Man, who claims that he is a descendant of the Gods, was making iron war, and his blood is being shed until the colour of the water is now crimson; this human is a victim of war."

63

The third one ventured, "I do not know what war is, but I do know that man, after having subdued the land, became aggressive and resolved to subdue the sea. He devised a strange object which carried him upon the seas, whereupon our severe Neptune became enraged over his greed. In order to please Neptune, man commenced offering gifts and sacrifices, and the still body before us is the most recent gift of man to our great and terrible Neptune."

The fourth one asserted, "How great is Neptune, and how cruel is his heart! If I were the Sultan of the sea I would refuse to accept such payment. . . . Come now, and let us examine this ransom. Perhaps we may enlighten ourselves as to the human clan."

The mermaids approached the youth, probed the pockets, and found a message close to his heart; one of them read it aloud to the others:

"My Beloved:
"Midnight has again come, and I have no consolation except my pouring tears, and naught to

comfort me save my hope in your return to me from between the bloody paws of war. I cannot forget your words when you took departure: 'Every man has a trust of tears which must be returned some day.'

"I know not what to say, My Beloved, but my soul will pour itself into parchment . . . my soul that suffers through separation, but is consoled by Love that renders pain a joy, and sorrow a happiness. When Love unified our hearts, and we looked to the day when our two hearts would be joined by the mighty breath of God, War shouted her horrible call and you followed her, prompted by your duty to the leaders.

"What is this duty that separates the lovers, and causes the women to become widows, and the children to become orphans? What is this patriotism which provokes wars and destroys kingdoms through trifles? And what cause can be more than trifling when compared to but one life? What is this duty which invites poor villagers, who are looked upon as nothing by the strong and by the sons of the inherited nobility, to die for the glory of

65

their oppressors? If duty destroys peace among nations, and patriotism disturbs the tranquility of man's life, then let us say, "Peace be with duty and patriotism."

"No, no, My Beloved! Heed not my words! Be courageous and faithful to your country.... Hearken not unto the talk of a damsel, blinded by Love, and lost through farewell and aloneness. . . . If Love will not restore you to me in this life, then Love will surely join us in the coming life.

Your Forever"

\*     \*     \*     \*     \*

The mermaids replaced the note under the youth's raiment and swam silently and sorrowfully away. As they gathered together at a distance from the body of the dead soldier, one of them said, "The human heart is more severe than the cruel heart of Neptune."

# We and You

# We and You

WE ARE THE SONS of Sorrow, and you are the
Sons of Joy. We are the sons of Sorrow,
And Sorrow is the shadow of a God who
Lives not in the domain of evil hearts.


We are sorrowful spirits, and Sorrow is
Too great to exist in small hearts.
When you laugh, we cry and lament; and he
Who is seared and cleansed once with his
Own tears will remain pure forevermore.


You understand us not, but we offer our
Sympathy to you. You are racing with the
Current of the River of Life, and you
Do not look upon us; but we are sitting by
The coast, watching you and hearing your
Strange voices.

You do not comprehend our cry, for the
Clamour of the days is crowding your ears,
Blocked with the hard substance of your
Years of indifference to truth; but we hear
Your songs, for the whispering of the night
Has opened our inner hearts. We see you
Standing under the pointing finger of light,
But you cannot see us, for we are tarrying
In the enlightening darkness.

We are the sons of Sorrow; we are the poets
And the prophets and the musicians. We weave
Raiment for the goddess from the threads of
Our hearts, and we fill the hands of the
Angels with the seeds of our inner selves.

You are the sons of the pursuit of earthly
Gaiety. You place your hearts in the hands
Of Emptiness, for the hand's touch to
Emptiness is smooth and inviting.

You reside in the house of Ignorance, for
In his house there is no mirror in which to
View your souls.

70

We sigh, and from our sighs arise the
Whispering of flowers and the rustling of
Leaves and the murmur of rivulets.


When you ridicule us your taunts mingle
With the crushing of the skulls and the
Rattling of shackles and the wailing of the
Abyss. When we cry, our tears fall into the
Heart of Life, as dew drops fall from the
Eyes of Night into the heart of Dawn; and
When you laugh, your mocking laughter pours
Down like the viper's venom into a wound.


We cry, and sympathize with the miserable
Wanderer and distressed widow; but you rejoice
And smile at the sight of resplendent gold.


We cry, for we listen to the moaning of the
Poor and the grieving of the oppressed weak;
But you laugh, for you hear naught but the
Happy sound of the wine goblets.

71

We cry, for our spirits are at the moment
Separated from God; but you laugh, for your
Bodies cling with unconcern to the earth.

*   *   *   *   *

We are the sons of Sorrow, and you are the
Sons of Joy. . . . Let us measure the outcome of
Our sorrow against the deeds of your joy
Before the face of the Sun. . . .


You have built the Pyramids upon the hearts
Of slaves, but the Pyramids stand now upon
The sand, commemorating to the Ages our
Immortality and your evanescence.


You have built Babylon upon the bones of the
Weak, and erected the palaces of Nineveh upon
The graves of the miserable. Babylon is now but
The footprint of the camel upon the moving sand
Of the desert, and its history is repeated
To the nations who bless us and curse you.

72

We have carved Ishtar from solid marble,
And made it to quiver in its solidity and
Speak through its muteness.

We have composed and played the soothing
Song of Nahawand upon the strings, and caused
The Beloved's spirit to come hovering in the
Firmament near to us; we have praised the
Supreme Being with words and deeds; the words
Became as the words of God, and the deeds
Became overwhelming love of the angels.

You are following Amusement, whose sharp claws
Have torn thousands of martyrs in the arenas
Of Rome and Antioch. . . . But we are following
Silence, whose careful fingers have woven the
Iliad and the Book of Job and the Lamentations
Of Jeremiah.

You lie down with Lust, whose tempest has
Swept one thousand processions of the soul of
Woman away and into the pit of shame and
Horror. . . . But we embrace Solitude, in whose
Shadow the beauties of Hamlet and Dante arose.

73

You curry for the favor of Greed, and the sharp
Swords of Greed have shed one thousand rivers
Of blood. . . . But we seek company with Truth,
And the hands of Truth have brought down
Knowledge from the Great Heart of the Circle
Of Light.

*　　*　　*　　*　　*

We are the sons of Sorrow, and you are the
Sons of Joy; and between our sorrow and your
Joy there is a rough and narrow path which
Your spirited horses cannot travel, and upon
Which your magnificent carriages cannot pass.

We pity your smallness as you hate our
Greatness; and between our pity and your
Hatred, Time halts bewildered. We come to
You as friends, but you attack us as enemies;
And between our friendship and your enmity,
There is a deep ravine flowing with tears
And blood.

74

We build palaces for you, and you dig graves
For us; and between the beauty of the palace
And the obscurity of the grave, Humanity
Walks as a sentry with iron weapons.

We spread your path with roses, and you cover
Our beds with thorns; and between the roses
And the thorns, Truth slumbers fitfully.

Since the beginning of the world you have
Fought against our gentle power with your
Coarse weakness; and when you triumph over
Us for an hour, you croak and clamour merrily
Like the frogs of the water. And when we
Conquer you and subdue you for an Age, we
Remain as silent giants.

\*　　\*　　\*　　\*　　\*

You crucified Jesus and stood below Him,
Blaspheming and mocking at Him; but at last
He came down and overcame the generations,
And walked among you as a hero, filling the
Universe with His glory and His beauty.

You poisoned Socrates and stoned Paul and
Destroyed Ali Talib and assassinated
Madhat Pasha, and yet those immortals are
With us forever before the face of Eternity.

But you live in the memory of man like
Corpses upon the face of the earth; and you
Cannot find a friend who will bury you in
The obscurity of non-existence and oblivion,
Which you sought on earth.

We are the sons of Sorrow, and sorrow is a
Rich cloud, showering the multitudes with
Knowledge and Truth. You are the sons of
Joy, and as high as your joy may reach,
By the Law of God it must be destroyed
Before the winds of heaven and dispersed
Into nothingness, for it is naught but a
Thin and wavering pillar of smoke.

# The Poet

# The Poet

I AM A STRANGER in this world, and there is a severe solitude and painful lonesomeness in my exile. I am alone, but in my aloneness I contemplate an unknown and enchanting country, and this meditation fills my dreams with spectres of a great and distant land which my eyes have never seen.

I am a stranger among my people and I have no friends. When I see a person I say within myself, "Who is he, and in what manner do I know him, and why is he here, and what law has joined me with him?"

I am a stranger to myself, and when I hear my tongue speak, my ears wonder over my voice; I see my inner self smiling, crying, braving, and fearing; and my existence wonders over my substance while my soul interrogates my heart; but I remain unknown, engulfed by tremendous silence.

My thoughts are strangers to my body, and as I stand before the mirror, I see something in my face which my soul does not see, and I find in my eyes what my inner self does not find.

When I walk vacant-eyed through the streets of the clamourous city, the children follow me, shouting, "Here is a blind man! Let us give him a walking cane to feel his way." When I run from them, I meet with a group of maidens, and they grasp the edges of my garment, saying, "He is deaf like the rock; let us fill his ears with the music of love." And when I flee from them, a throng of aged people point at me with trembling fingers and say, "He is a madman who lost his mind in the world of genii and ghouls."

*     *     *     *     *

I am a stranger in this world; I roamed the Universe from end to end, but could not find a place to rest my head; nor did I know any human I confronted, neither an individual who would hearken to my mind.

When I open my sleepless eyes at dawn, I find

myself imprisoned in a dark cave from whose ceiling hang the insects and upon whose floor crawl the vipers.

When I go out to meet the light, the shadow of my body follows me, but the shadow of my spirit precedes me and leads the way to an unknown place seeking things beyond my understanding, and grasping objects that are meaningless to me.

At eventide I return and lie upon my bed, made of soft feathers and lined with thorns, and I contemplate and feel the troublesome and happy desires, and sense the painful and joyous hopes.

At midnight the ghosts of the past ages and the spirits of the forgotten civilization enter through the crevices of the cave to visit me . . . I stare at them and they gaze upon me; I talk to them and they answer me smilingly. Then I endeavour to clutch them, but they sift through my fingers and vanish like the mist which rests on the lake.

\*     \*     \*     \*     \*

I am a stranger in this world, and there is no one in the Universe who understands the language I speak. Patterns of bizarre remembrance form suddenly in my mind, and my eyes bring forth queer images and sad ghosts. I walk in the deserted prairies, watching the streamlets running fast, up and up from the depths of the valley to the top of the mountain; I watch the naked trees blooming and bearing fruit, and shedding their leaves in one instant, and then I see the branches fall and turn into speckled snakes. I see the birds hovering above, singing and wailing; then they stop and open their wings and turn into undraped maidens with long hair, looking at me from behind kohled and infatuated eyes, and smiling at me with full lips soaked with honey, stretching their scented hands toward me. Then they ascend and disappear from my sight like phantoms, leaving in the firmament the resounding echo of their taunts and mocking laughter.

I am a stranger in this world . . . I am a poet who composes what life proses, and who proses what life composes.

For this reason I am a stranger, and I shall remain a stranger until the white and friendly wings of Death carry me home into my beautiful country. There, where light and peace and understanding abide, I will await the other strangers who will be rescued by the friendly trap of time from this narrow, dark world.

Ashes of the Ages and Eternal Fire

# Ashes of the Ages and Eternal Fire

## PART I

### Spring of the Year 116 B.C.

NIGHT HAD FALLEN and silence prevailed while life slumbered in the City of the Sun,* and the lamps were extinguished in the scattered houses about the majestic temples amidst the olive and laurel trees. The moon poured its silver rays upon the white marble columns that stood like giants in the silence of the night, guarding the gods' temples and looking with perplexity toward the towers of Lebanon that sat bristling upon the foreheads of the distant hills.

---

* Baalbek, or the City of Baal, called by the ancients "The City of the Sun," was built in honor of the Sun God Heliopolis, and historians assert that Baalbek was the most beautiful city in the Middle East. Its ruins, which we observe at present time, indicate that the architecture was largely influenced by the Romans during the occupation of Syria. (Editor's note.)

At that hour, while souls succumbed to the allure of slumber, Nathan, the son of the High Priest, entered Ishtar's temple, bearing a torch in trembling hands. He lighted the lamps and censers until the aromatic scent of myrrh and frankincense reached to the farthest corners; then he knelt before the altar, studded with inlays of ivory and gold, raised his hands toward Ishtar, and with a painful and choking voice he cried out, saying, "Have mercy upon me, O great Ishtar, goddess of Love and Beauty. Be merciful, and remove the hands of Death from my beloved, whom my soul has chosen by thy will. . . . The potions of the physicians and the wizards do not restore her life, neither the enchantments of the priests and the sorcerers. Naught is left to be done except thy holy will. Thou art my guide and my aid. Have mercy on me and grant my prayers! * Gaze upon my crushed heart and aching soul! Spare my beloved's

---

* Ishtar was the great goddess of the Phoenicians. They worshipped her in the cities of Tyre, Sidon, Sûr, Djabeil and Baalbek, and described her as the Burner of the Torch of Life, and Guardian of Youth. Greece adored her after Phoenicia, calling her the goddess of Love and Beauty. The Romans called her Venus. (Editor's note.)

life so that we may rejoice with the secrets of thy love, and glory in the beauty of youth that reveals the mystery of thy strength and wisdom. From the depths of my heart I cry unto thee, O exalted Ishtar, and from behind the darkness of the night I beg thy mercy; hear me, O Ishtar! I am thy good servant Nathan, the son of the High Priest Hiram, and I devote all of my deeds and words to thy greatness at thy altar.

"I love a maiden amongst all maidens and made her my companion, but the genii brides envied her and blew into her body a strange affliction and sent unto her the messenger of Death who is standing by her bed like a hungry spectre, spreading his black ribbed wings over her, stretching forth his sharp claws in readiness to prey upon her. I come here now beseeching you to have mercy upon me and spare that flower who has not yet rejoiced with the summer of Life.

"Save her from the grasp of Death so we may sing joyfully thy praise and burn incense in thine honour and offer sacrifices at thy altar, filling thy vases with perfumed oil and spreading roses and violets upon the portico of thy place of worship, burning frankincense before thy shrine. Save her, O Ishtar, goddess of miracles, and let Love overcome Death in this struggle of Joy against Sorrow." *

Nathan then became silent. His eyes were flooded with tears and his heart was uttering sorrowful sighs; then he continued, "Alas, my dreams are shattered, O Ishtar divine, and my heart is melted within; enliven me with thy mercy and spare my beloved."

At that moment one of his slaves entered the temple, hastened to Nathan, and whispered to him, "She has opened her eyes, Master, and looked about her bed, but could not find you; then she called for you, and I used all speed to advise you."

Nathan departed hurriedly and the slave followed him.

---

* During the Era of Ignorance, the Arabs believed that if a genie loved a human youth, she would prevent him from marrying, and if he did wed, she would bewitch the bride and cause her to die. This mythological superstition persists today in some small villages in Lebanon. (Editor's note.)

When he reached his palace, he entered the chamber of the ailing maiden, leaned over her bed, held her frail hand, and printed several kisses upon her lips as if striving to breathe into her body a new life from his own life. She moved her head on the silk cushions and opened her eyes. And upon her lips appeared the phantom of a smile which was the faint residue of life in her wasted body . . . the echo of the calling of a heart which is racing toward a halt; and with a voice that bespoke the weakening cries of a hungry infant on the breast of a withered mother, she said, "The goddess has called me, Oh Life of my Soul, and Death has come to sever me from you; but fear not, for the will of the goddess is sacred, and the demands of Death are just. I am departing now, and I hear the rustle of the whiteness descending, but the cups of Love and Youth are still full in our hands, and the flowered paths of beautiful Life are extended before us. I am embarking, My Beloved, upon an ark of the spirit, and I shall come back to this world, for great Ishtar will bring back to life those souls of loving humans who departed to

Eternity before they enjoyed the sweetness of Love and the happiness of Youth.

"We shall meet again, Oh Nathan, and drink together the dew of the dawn from the cupped petals of the lilies, and rejoice with the birds of the fields over the colours of the rainbow. Until then, My Forever, farewell." *

Her voice lowered and her lips trembled like a lone flower before the gusts of dawn. Nathan embraced her with pouring tears, and as he pressed his lips upon her lips, he found them cold as the stone of the field. He uttered a terrible cry and commenced tearing his raiment; he threw himself upon her dead body while his shivering soul was sailing fitfully between the mountain of Life and the precipice of Death.

In the silence of the night, the slumbering souls were awakened. Women and children were

---

* Many Asiatics pursue this belief with conviction, having derived it from their holy writings. Mohammed said, "You were dead and He brought you back to life, and He will deaden you again and then will enliven you, whereupon you shall go back to Him." Buddha said, "Yesterday we existed in this life, and now we came, and we will continue to go back until we become perfect like the God." (Editor's note.)

frightened as they heard mighty rumbling and painful wailing and bitter lamentation coming from the corners of the palace of the High Priest of Ishtar.

When the tired morn arrived, the people asked about Nathan to offer their sympathy, but were told that he had disappeared. And after a fort-night, the chief of a caravan arriving from the East related that he had seen Nathan in the distant wilderness, wandering with a flock of gazelles.

*     *     *     *     *

The ages passed, crushing with their invisible feet the feeble acts of the civilizations, and the goddess of Love and Beauty had left the country. A strange and fickle goddess took her place. She destroyed the magnificent temples of the City of the Sun and demolished its beautiful palaces. The blooming orchards and fertile prairies were laid waste and nothing was left in that spot save ruins commemorating to the aching souls the ghosts of Yesterday, repeating to the sorrowful spirits only the echo of the hymns of glory.

93

But the severe ages that crushed the deeds of man could not destroy his dreams; nor could they weaken his love, for dreams and affections are ever-living with the Eternal Spirit. They may disappear for a time, pursuing the sun when the night comes, and the stars when morning appears, but like the lights of heaven, they must surely return.

## PART II

### *Spring of the Year 1890 A.D.*

The day was over, Nature was making her many preparations for slumber, and the sun withdrew its golden rays from the plains of Baalbek. Ali El Hosseini * brought his herd back to the shed in the midst of the ruins of the temples. He sat there near the ancient columns which symbolized the bones of countless soldiers left behind in the field of battle. The sheep folded around him, charmed with the music of his flute.

---

* The Hosseinese are groups comprising an Arabian tribe, at present living in tents pitched in the plains surrounding the ruins of Baalbek. (Editor's note.)

Midnight came, and heaven sowed the seeds of the following day in the deep furrows of the darkness. Ali's eyes became tired of the phantoms of awakeness, and his mind was wearied by the procession of ghosts marching in horrible silence amidst the demolished walls. He leaned upon his arm, and sleep captured his senses with the extreme end of its plaited veil, like a delicate cloud touching the face of a calm lake. He forgot his actual self and encountered his invisible self, rich with dreams and ideals higher than the laws and teachings of man. The circle of vision broadened before his eyes, and Life's hidden secrets gradually became apparent to him. His soul abandoned the rapid parade of time rushing toward nothingness; it stood alone before symmetrical thoughts and crystal ideas. For the first time in his life, Ali was aware of the causes for the spiritual famine that had accompanied his youth. . . . The famine which levels away the pit between the sweetness and the bitterness of Life. . . . That thirst which unites into contentment the sighs of Affection and the silence of Satisfaction. . . . That longing

95

which cannot be vanquished by the glory of the world nor twisted by the passing of the ages. Ali felt the surge of a strange affection and a kind tenderness within himself which was Memory, enlivening itself like incense placed upon white firebrands. . . . It was a magic love whose soft fingers had touched Ali's heart as a musician's delicate fingers touch quivering strings. It was a new power emanating from nothingness and growing forcefully, embracing his real self and filling his spirit with ardent love, at once painful and sweet.

Ali looked toward the ruins and his heavy eyes became alert as he fancied the glory of those devastated shrines that stood as mighty, impregnable, and eternal temples long before. His eyes became motionless and the breathing of his heart quickened. And like a blind man whose sight has suddenly been restored, he commenced to see, think and meditate. . . . He recollected the lamps and the silver censers that surrounded the image of an adored and revered goddess. . . . He remembered the priests offering sacrifices before an altar built of ivory and gold. . . . He envisioned the dancing maidens, and the tambourine players, and the singers who chanted the praise of the goddess of Love and Beauty; he saw all this before him, and felt the impression of their obscurity in the choking depths of his heart.

But memory alone brings naught save echoes of voices heard in the depths of the long ago. What, then, is the bizarre relationship between these powerful, weaving memories and the past actual life of a simple youth who was born in a tent and who spent the spring of his life grazing sheep in the valleys?

Ali gathered himself and walked amidst the ruins, and the gnawing memories suddenly tore the veil of oblivion from his thoughts. As he reached the great and cavernous entrance to the temple, he halted as if a magnetic power gripped him and fastened his feet. As he looked downward, he found a smashed statue on the ground. He broke from the grasp of the Unseen and at once his soul's tears unleashed and poured like blood issuing from a deep wound; his heart roared in ebb and flow like the welling waves of the sea.

97

He sighed bitterly and cried painfully, for he felt a stabbing aloneness and a destructive remoteness standing as an abyss between his heart and the heart from whom he was torn before he entered upon this life. He felt that his soul's element was but a flame from the burning torch which God had separated from Himself before the passing of the Ages. He perceived the feathery touch of delicate wings rustling about his flaming heart, and a great love possessing him. . . . A love whose power separates the mind from the world of quantity and measurement. . . . A love that talks when the tongue of Life is muted. . . . A love that stands as a blue beacon to point out the path, guiding with no visible light. That love or that God who descended in that quiet hour upon Ali's heart had seared into his being a bitter and sweet affection, like thorns growing by the side of the flourishing flowers.

But who is this Love and whence did he come? What does he desire of a shepherd kneeling in the midst of those ruins? Is it a seed sown without awareness in the domain of the heart by a Bedouin maiden? Or a beam appeared from behind the dark cloud to illuminate life? Is it a dream that crept close in the silence of the night to ridicule him? Or is it Truth that existed since the Beginning, and shall continue to exist until the Ending?

Ali closed his tearful eyes and stretched forth his arms like a beggar, and exclaimed, "Who are you, standing close to my heart but away from my sight, yet acting as a great wall between me and my real self, binding my today with my forgotten past? Are you the phantom of a spectre from Eternity to show me the vanity of Life and the weakness of mankind? Or the spirit of a genie appeared from the earth's crevices to enslave me and render me an object of mockery amongst the youths of my tribe? Who are you and what is this strange power which at one time deadens and enlivens my heart? Who am I and what is this strange self whom I call "Myself"? Has the Water of Life which I drank made of me an angel, seeing and hearing the mysterious secrets of the Universe, or is it merely an evil wine that intoxicated me and blinded me from myself?"

He became silent, while his anxiety grew and his spirit exulted. Then he continued, "Oh, that which the soul reveals, and the night conceals. . . . Oh, beautiful spirit, hovering in the sky of my dream; you have awakened in me a dormant fullness, like healthy seeds hidden under the blankets of snow; you have passed me like a frolicsome breeze carrying to my hungry self the fragrance of the flowers of heaven; you have touched my senses and agitated and quivered them like the leaves of the trees. Let me look upon you now if you are a human, or command Slumber to shut my eyes so I can view your vastness through my inner being. Let me touch you; let me hear your voice. Tear away this veil that conceals my entire purpose, and destroy this wall that hides my deity from my clearing eyes, and place upon me a pair of wings so I may fly behind you to the halls of the Supreme Universe. Or bewitch my eyes so I may follow you to the ambush of the genii if you are one of their brides. If I am worthy, place your hand upon my heart and possess me."

Ali was whispering these words into the mystic

100

darkness, and before him crept the ghosts of night, as if they were vapour coming from his boiling tears. Upon the walls of the temple he fancied magical pictures painted with the brush of the rainbow.

Thus did one hour pass, with Ali shedding tears and reveling in his miserable plight and hearing the beats of his heart, looking beyond the objects as if he were observing the images of Life vanishing slowly and being replaced with a dream, strange in its beauty and terrible in enormity. Like a prophet who meditates the stars of heaven awaiting the Descent and Revelation, he pondered the power existing beyond these contemplations. He felt that his spirit left him and probed through the temples for a priceless but unknown segment of himself, lost among the ruins.

Dawn had appeared and silence roared with the passing of the breeze; the first rays of light raced through, illuminating the particles of the ether, and the sky smiled like a dreamer viewing his beloved's phantom. The birds probed from their sanctuary in the crevices of the walls and emerged into the halls of the columns, singing their morning prayers.

Ali placed his cupped hand over his forehead, looking downward with glazed eyes. Like Adam, when God opened his eyes with Almighty breath, Ali saw new objects, strange and fantastic. Then he approached his sheep and called to them, whereupon they followed him quietly toward the lush fields. He led them, as he gazed at the sky like a philosopher divining and meditating the secrets of the Universe. He reached a brook whose murmuring was soothing to the spirit, and he sat by the edge of the spring under the willow tree, whose branches dipped over the water as if drinking from the cool depths. The dew of dawn glistened upon the sheep's wood as they grazed amid flowers and green grass.

In a few moments Ali again felt that his heartbeats were increasing rapidly and his spirit commenced to vibrate violently, almost visibly. Like a mother suddenly awakened from her slumber by the scream of her child, he bolted from his position, and as his eyes were compelled to her, he saw a beautiful maiden carrying an earthenware container upon her shoulder, slowly approaching the far side of the brook. As she reached the edge and leaned forward to fill the jar, she glanced across, and her eyes met Ali's eyes. As if in insanity she cried out, dropped the jar, and withdrew swiftly. Then she turned, gazing at Ali with anxious, agonizing disbelief.

A minute passed, whose seconds were glittering lamps illuminating their hearts and spirits, and silence brought vague remembrance, revealing to them images and scenes far away from that brook and those trees. They heard each other in the understanding silence, listening tearfully to each other's sighs of heart and soul until complete knowing prevailed between the two.

Ali, still compelled by a mysterious power, leaped across the brook and approached the maiden, embraced her and printed a long kiss upon her lips. As if the sweetness of Ali's caress had usurped her will, she did not move, and the kind touch of Ali's arms had stolen her strength. She yielded to him as the fragrance of jasmine concedes to the vibration of the breeze, carrying it into the spacious firmament.

She placed her head upon his chest like a tortured person who has found rest. She sighed deeply. . . . a sigh that announced the rebirth of happiness in a torn heart and proclaimed a revolution of wings that had ascended after having been injured and committed to earth.

She raised her head and looked at him with her soul. . . . the look of a human which, in mighty silence, belittles the conventional words used amongst mankind; the expression which offers myriads of thoughts in the unspoken language of the hearts. She bore the look of a person who accepts Love not as a spirit in a body of words, but as a reunion occurring long after two souls were divided by earth and joined by God.

The enamoured couple walked amidst the willow trees, and the singleness of two selves was a speaking tongue for their unification; a seeing eye for the glory of Happiness; a silent listener to the tremendous revelation of Love.

The sheep continued grazing, and the birds of

the sky still hovered above their heads, singing the song of Dawn, following the emptiness of night. As they reached the end of the valley the sun appeared, spreading a golden garment upon the knolls and the hills, and they sat by the side of a rock where the violets hid. The maiden looked into Ali's black eyes while the breeze caressed her hair, as if the shimmering wisps were fingertips craving for sweet kisses. She felt as though some magic and strong gentleness were touching her lips in spite of her will, and with a serene and charming voice she said, "Ishtar has restored both of our spirits to this life from another, so we may not be denied the joy of Love and the glory of Youth, my beloved."

Ali closed his eyes, as if her musical voice brought to him images of a dream he had seen, and he felt an invisible pair of wings carrying him from that place and depositing him in a strange chamber by the side of a bed upon which lay the corpse of a maiden whose beauty had been claimed by Death. He cried fearfully, then opened his eyes and found that same maiden sitting by his side, and upon her lips appeared a smile. Her eyes shone with the rays of Life. Ali's face brightened and his heart was refreshed. The phantom of his vision withdrew slowly until he forgot completely the past and its cares. The two lovers embraced and drank the wine of sweet kisses together until they became intoxicated. They slumbered, wrapped between each other's arms, until the last remnant of the shadow was dispersed by the Eternal Power which had awakened them.

# Between Night and Morn

# Between Night and Morn

Be silent, my heart, for the space cannot
Hear you; be silent, for the ether is
Laden with cries and moans, and cannot
Carry your songs and hymns.

Be silent, for the phantoms of the night
Will not give heed to the whispering of
Your secrets; nor will the processions
Of darkness halt before your dreams.

Be silent, my heart, until Dawn comes,
For he who patiently awaits the morn
Will meet him surely, and he who loves
The light will be loved by the light.

Be silent, my heart, and hearken to my
Story; in my dream I saw a nightingale
Singing over the throat of a fiery
Volcano, and I saw a lily raising her

Head above the snow, and a naked Houri
Dancing in the midst of the graves, and
An infant playing with skulls while
Laughing.

I saw all these images in my dream, and
When I opened my eyes and looked about
Me, I saw the volcano still raging, but
No longer heard the nightingale sing;
Nor did I see him hovering.

I saw the sky spreading snow upon the
Fields and valleys, and concealing under
White shrouds the stilled bodies of the
Lilies. I saw a row of graves before
The silence of the Ages, but there was
No person dancing or praying in their
Midst. I saw a heap of skulls, but no
One was there to laugh, save the wind.

In my awakeness I saw grief and sorrow;
What became of the joy and sweetness of
My dream? Where has the beauty of my
Dream gone, and in what manner did the
Images disappear?

110

How can the soul be patient until Slumber
Restores the happy phantoms of hope and
Desire?

Give heed, my heart, and hear my story;
Yesterday my soul was like an old and
Strong tree, whose roots grasped into the
Depths of the earth, and whose branches
Reached the Infinite. My soul blossomed
In Spring, and gave fruit in Summer, and
When Autumn came, I gathered the fruit on
A silver tray and placed it by the
Walker's portion of the street; and all
Who passed partook willingly and continued
To walk.

And when Autumn passed away, and submerged
His rejoicing under wailing and lamentation,
I looked upon my tray and found but one
Fruit remaining; I took it and placed it
Into my mouth, but found it bitter as gall,
And sour as the hard grapes, and I said to
Myself, "Woe to me, for I have placed a

III

Curse in the mouths of the people, and an
Ailment in their bodies. What have you
Done, my soul, with the sweet sap which
Your roots have sucked from the earth, and
The fragrance which you have drawn from
The sky?" In anger did I tear the strong
And old tree of my soul, with each of the
Struggling roots, from the depths of the
Earth.

I uprooted it from the past, and took
From it the memories of one thousand
Springs and one thousand Autumns, and I
Planted the tree of my soul in another
Place. It was now in a field afar from
The path of Time; and I tended it in day
And in night, saying within me, "Wakefulness
Will bring us closer to the stars."

I watered it with blood and tears, saying,
"There is a flavour in blood, and a
Sweetness in tears." When Spring returned,
My tree bloomed again, and in the Summer it

Bore fruit. And when Autumn came, I gathered
All the ripe fruit upon a golden plate and
Offered it in the public path, and the people
Passed but none desired my fruit.

Then I took one fruit and brought it to my
Lips, and it was sweet as the honeycomb
And exhilarating as the wine of Babylon
And fragrant as the jasmine. And I cried
Out, saying, "The people do not want a
Blessing in their mouths, nor a truth in
Their hearts, for Blessing is the daughter
Of Tears, and Truth is the son of Blood."

I left the noisome city to sit in the shadow
Of the solitary tree of my soul, in a
Field far from life's path.

\*    \*    \*    \*    \*

Be silent, my heart, until Dawn comes;
Be silent and attend my story;
Yesterday my thoughts were a boat sailing
Amidst the waves in the sea, and moving

With the winds from one land to another.
And my boat was empty except of seven
Jars of rainbow colours; and the time
Came when I grew weary of moving about
On the face of the sea, and I said to
Myself, "I shall return with the empty
Boat of my thoughts to the harbour of the
Isle of my birth."

And I prepared by colouring my boat yellow
Like the sunset, and green like the heart
Of Spring, and blue like the sky, and red
Like the anemone. And on the masts and
On the rudder I drew strange figures that
Compelled the attention and dazzled the
Eye. And as I ended my task, the boat of
My thoughts seemed as a prophetic vision,
Sailing between the two infinities, the
Sea and the sky.

I entered the harbour of the isle of my
Birth, and the people surged to meet me
With singing and merriment. And the

114

Throngs invited me to enter the city;
And they were plucking their instruments
And sounding their tambourines.

Such welcome was mine because my boat
Was beautifully decorated, and none
Entered and saw the interior of the
Boat of my thoughts, nor asked what
I had brought from beyond the seas. Nor
Could they observe that I had brought
My boat back empty, for its brilliance
Had rendered them blind. Thereupon I
Said within myself, "I have led the
People astray, and with seven jars of
Colours I have cheated their eyes."

Thereafter, I embarked in the boat of
My thoughts, again to set sail. I
Visited the East Islands and gathered
Myrrh, frankincense and sandalwood, and
Placed them in my boat. . . . I roamed the
West Islands and brought ivory and ruby
And emerald and many rare gems. . . . I

Journeyed the South Islands and carried
Back with me beautiful armours and
Glittering swords and spears and all
Varieties of weapons. . . . I filled the
Boat of my thoughts with the choicest
And most precious things on earth, and
Returned to the harbour of the isle of
My birth, saying, "The people shall again
Glorify me, but with honesty, and they
Shall again invite me to enter their
City, but with merit."

And when I reached the harbour, none
Came to meet me. . . . I walked the streets
Of my earlier glory but no person looked
Upon me. . . . I stood in the market place
Shouting to the people of the treasures
In my boat, and they mocked at me and
Heeded not.

I returned to the harbour with spiritless
Heart and disappointment and confusion.
And when I gazed upon my boat, I observed

A thing which I had not seen during my
Voyage, and I exclaimed, "The waves of
The sea have done away with the colours and
The figures on my boat and caused it to look
Like a skeleton." The winds and the spray
Together with the burning sun had effaced
The brilliant hues and my boat looked now
Like tattered grey raiment. I could not
Observe these changes from amid my treasures,
For I had blinded my eyes from the inside.

I had gathered the most precious things on
Earth and placed them in a floating chest
Upon the face of the water and returned to
My people, but they cast me away and could
Not see me, for their eyes had been allured
By empty, shimmering objects.

At that hour I left the boat of my thoughts
For the City of the Dead, and sat in the
Midst of the trim graves, contemplating
Their secrets.

\*     \*     \*     \*     \*

Be silent, my heart, until Dawn comes; be
Silent, for the raging tempest is ridiculing
Your inner whispering, and the caves of
The valleys do not echo the vibration of
Your strings.

Be silent, my heart, until Morn comes,
For he who awaits patiently the coming
Of Dawn will be embraced longingly by
Morningtide.

Dawn is breaking. Speak if you are able,
My heart. Here is the procession of
Morningtide. . . . Why do you not speak?
Has not the silence of the night left
A song in your inner depths with which
You may meet Dawn?

Here are the swarms of doves and the
Nightingales moving in the far portion
Of the valley. Are you capable of flying
With the birds, or has the horrible night
Weakened your wings? The shepherds are

118

Leading the sheep from their folds; has
The phantom of the night left strength
In you so you may walk behind them to
The green prairies? The young men and
Women are walking gracefully toward the
Vineyards. Will you be able to stand
And walk with them? Rise, my heart, and
Walk with Dawn, for the night has passed,
And the fear of darkness has vanished with
Its black dreams and ghastly thoughts and
Insane travels.

Rise, my heart, and raise your voice with
Music, for he who shares not Dawn with
His songs is one of the sons of ever-
Darkness.

# The Secrets of the Heart

# The Secrets of the Heart

A MAJESTIC MANSION stood under the wings of
the silent night, as Life stands under the cover of
Death. In it sat a maiden at an ivory desk, leaning
her beautiful head on her soft hand, as a withering
lily leans upon its petals. She looked around, feeling like a miserable prisoner, struggling to penetrate the walls of the dungeon with her eyes in
order to witness Life walking in the procession of
Freedom.

The hours passed like the ghosts of the night,
as a procession chanting the dirge of her sorrow,
and the maiden felt secure with the shedding of
her tears in anguished solitude. When she could
not resist the pressure of her suffering any longer,
and as she felt that she was in full possession of the
treasured secrets of her heart, she took the quill
and commenced mingling her tears with ink upon
parchment, and she inscribed:

"My Beloved Sister,

"When the heart becomes congested with secrets, and the eyes begin to burn from the searing tears, and the ribs are about to burst with the growing of the heart's confinement, one cannot find expression for such a labyrinth except by a surge of release.

"Sorrowful persons find joy in lamentation, and lovers encounter comfort and condolence in dreams, and the oppressed delight in receiving sympathy. I am writing to you now because I feel like a poet who fancies the beauty of objects whose impression he composes in verse while being ruled by a divine power. . . . I am like a child of the starving poor who cries for food, instigated by bitterness of hunger, disregarding the plight of his poor and merciful mother and her defeat in life.

"Listen to my painful story, my dear sister, and weep with me, for sobbing is like a prayer, and the tears of mercy are like a charity because they come forth from a living and sensitive and good soul and they are not shed in vain. It was the will of my father when I married a noble and rich man. My

124

father was like most of the rich, whose only joy in life is to improve their wealth by adding more gold to their coffers in fear of poverty, and curry nobility with grandeur in anticipation of the attacks of the black days. . . . I find myself now, with all my love and dreams, a victim upon a golden altar which I hate, and an inherited honour which I despise.

"I respect my husband because he is generous and kind to all; he endeavours to bring happiness to me, and spends his gold to please my heart, but I have found that the impression of all these things is not worth one moment of a true and divine love. Do not ridicule me, my sister, for I am now a most enlightened person regarding the needs of a woman's heart—that throbbing heart which is like a bird flying in the spacious sky of love. . . . It is like a vase replenished with the wine of the ages that has been pressed for the sipping souls. . . . It is like a book in whose pages one reads the chapters of happiness and misery, joy and pain, laughter and sorrow. No one can read this book except the true companion who is the other half of the woman, created for her since the beginning of the world.

"Yes, I became most knowing amongst all women as to the purpose of the soul and meaning of the heart, for I have found that my magnificent horses and beautiful carriages and glittering coffers of gold and sublime nobility are not worth one glance from the eyes of that poor young man who is patiently waiting and suffering the pangs of bitterness and misery. . . . That youth who is oppressed by the cruelty and will of my father, and imprisoned in the narrow and melancholy jail of Life. . . .

"Please, my dear, do not contrive to console me, for the calamity through which I have realized the power of my love is my great consoler. Now I am looking forward from behind my tears and awaiting the coming of Death to lead me to where I will meet the companion of my soul and embrace him as I did before we entered this strange world.

"Do not think evil of me, for I am doing my duty as a faithful wife, and complying calmly and

126

patiently with the laws and rules of man. I honour my husband with my sense, and respect him with my heart, and revere him with my soul, but there is a withholding, for God gave part of me to my beloved before I knew him.

"Heaven willed that I spend my life with a man not meant for me, and I am wasting my days silently according to the will of Heaven; but if the gates of Eternity do not open, I will remain with the beautiful half of my soul and look back to the Past, and that Past is this Present. . . . I shall look at life as Spring looks at Winter, and contemplate the obstacles of Life as one who has climbed the rough trail and reached the mountain top."

\* \* \* \* \*

At that moment the maiden ceased writing and hid her face with her cupped hands and wept bitterly. Her heart declined to entrust to the pen its most sacred secrets, but resorted to the pouring of dry tears that dispersed quickly and mingled with the gentle ether, the haven of the lovers' souls and the flowers' spirits. After a moment she took the quill and added, "Do you remember that youth? Do you recollect the rays which emanated from his eyes, and the sorrowful signs upon his face? Do you recall that laughter which bespoke the tears of a mother, torn from her only child? Can you retrace his serene voice speaking the echo of a distant valley? Do you remember him meditating and staring longingly and calmly at objects and speaking of them in strange words, and then bending his head and sighing as if fearing to reveal the secrets of his great heart? Do you recall his dreams and beliefs? Do you recollect all these things in a youth whom humanity counts as one of her children and upon whom my father looked with eyes of superiority because he is higher than earthly greed and nobler than inherited grandeur?

"You know, my dear sister, that I am a martyr in this belittling world, and a victim of ignorance. Will you sympathize with a sister who sits in the silence of the horrible night pouring down the contents of her inner self and revealing to you her heart's secrets? I am sure that you will sympathize

128

with me, for I know that Love has visited your
heart."

*    *    *    *    *

Dawn came, and the maiden surrendered herself to Slumber, hoping to find sweeter and more
gentle dreams than those she had encountered
in her awakeness. . . .

# My Countrymen

# My Countrymen

WHAT DO YOU SEEK, My Countrymen?
Do you desire that I build for
You gorgeous palaces, decorated
With words of empty meaning, or
Temples roofed with dreams? Or
Do you command me to destroy what
The liars and tyrants have built?
Shall I uproot with my fingers
What the hypocrites and the wicked
Have implanted? Speak your insane
Wish!

What is it you would have me do,
My Countrymen? Shall I purr like
The kitten to satisfy you, or roar
Like the lion to please myself? I
Have sung for you, but you did not
Dance; I have wept before you, but

You did not cry. Shall I sing and
Weep at the same time?


Your souls are suffering the pangs
Of hunger, and yet the fruit of
Knowledge is more plentiful than
The stones of the valleys.


Your hearts are withering from
Thirst, and yet the springs of
Life are streaming about your
Homes—why do you not drink?
The sea has its ebb and flow,
The moon has its fullness and
Crescents, and the Ages have
Their winter and summer, and all
Things vary like the shadow of
An unborn God moving between
Earth and sun, but Truth cannot
Be changed, nor will it pass away;
Why, then, do you endeavour to
Disfigure its countenance?

I have called you in the silence
Of the night to point out the
Glory of the moon and the dignity
Of the stars, but you startled
From your slumber and clutched
Your swords in fear, crying,
"Where is the enemy? We must kill
Him first!" At morningtide, when
The enemy came, I called to you
Again, but now you did not wake
From your slumber, for you were
Locked in fear, wrestling with
The processions of spectres in
Your dreams.

And I said unto you, "Let us climb
To the mountain top and view the
Beauty of the world." And you
Answered me, saying, "In the depths
Of this valley our fathers lived,
And in its shadow they died, and in
Its caves they were buried. How can

We depart this place for one which
They failed to honour?"

And I said unto you, "Let us go to
The plain that gives its bounty to
The sea." And you spoke timidly to
Me, saying, "The uproar of the abyss
Will frighten our spirits, and the
Terror of the depths will deaden
Our bodies."

*　　*　　*　　*　　*

I have loved you, My Countrymen, but
My love for you is painful to me
And useless to you; and today I
Hate you, and hatred is a flood
That sweeps away the dry branches
And quavering houses.

I have pitied your weakness, My
Countrymen, but my pity has but
Increased your feebleness, exalting
And nourishing slothfulness which

Is vain to Life. And today I see
Your infirmity which my soul loathes
And fears.

I have cried over your humiliation
And submission; and my tears streamed
Like crystalline, but could not sear
Away your stagnant weakness; yet they
Removed the veil from my eyes.

My tears have never reached your
Petrified hearts, but they cleansed
The darkness from my inner self.
Today I am mocking at your suffering,
For laughter is a raging thunder that
Precedes the tempest and never comes
After it.

What do you desire, My Countrymen?
Do you wish for me to show you
The ghost of your countenance on
The face of still water? Come,
Now, and see how ugly you are!

Look and meditate! Fear has
Turned your hair grey as the
Ashes, and dissipation has grown
Over your eyes and made them into
Obscured hollows, and cowardice
Has touched your cheeks that now
Appear as dismal pits in the
Valley, and Death has kissed
Your lips and left them yellow
As the Autumn leaves.

What is it that you seek, My
Countrymen? What ask you from
Life, who does not any longer
Count you among her children?

Your souls are freezing in the
Clutches of the priests and
Sorcerers, and your bodies
Tremble between the paws of the
Despots and the shedders of
Blood, and your country quakes
Under the marching feet of the

Conquering enemy; what may you
Expect even though you stand
Proudly before the face of the
Sun? Your swords are sheathed
With rust, and your spears are
Broken, and your shields are
Laden with gaps; why, then, do
You stand in the field of battle?

Hypocrisy is your religion, and
Falsehood is your life, and
Nothingness is your ending; why,
Then, are you living? Is not
Death the sole comfort of the
Miserables?

\*     \*     \*     \*     \*

Life is a resolution that
Accompanies youth, and a diligence
That follows maturity, and a
Wisdom that pursues senility; but
You, My Countrymen, were born old
And weak. And your skins withered

139

And your heads shrank, whereupon
You became as children, running
Into the mire and casting stones
Upon each other.

Knowledge is a light, enriching
The warmth of life, and all may
Partake who seek it out; but you,
My Countrymen, seek out darkness
And flee the light, awaiting the
Coming of water from the rock,
And your nation's misery is your
Crime. . . . I do not forgive you
Your sins, for you know what you
Are doing.

Humanity is a brilliant river
Singing its way and carrying with
It the mountains' secrets into
The heart of the sea; but you,
My Countrymen, are stagnant
Marshes infested with insects
And vipers.

The Spirit is a sacred blue
Torch, burning and devouring
The dry plants, and growing
With the storm and illuminating
The faces of the goddesses; but
You, My Countrymen . . . your souls
Are like ashes which the winds
Scatter upon the snow, and which
The tempests disperse forever in
The valleys.

Fear not the phantom of Death,
My Countrymen, for his greatness
And mercy will refuse to approach
Your smallness; and dread not the
Dagger, for it will decline to be
Lodged in your shallow hearts.

I hate you, My Countrymen, because
You hate glory and greatness. I
Despise you because you despise
Yourselves. I am your enemy, for
You refuse to realize that you are
The enemies of the goddesses.

John the Madman

# John the Madman

IN SUMMER John walked every morning into the field, driving his oxen and carrying his plough over his shoulder, hearkening to the soothing songs of the birds and the rustling of the leaves and the grass.

At noon he sat beside a brook in the colourful prairies for repast, leaving a few morsels upon the green grass for the birds of the sky.

At eventide he returned to his wretched hovel that stood apart from those hamlets and villages in North Lebanon. After the evening meal he sat and listened attentively to his parents, who related tales of the past ages until sleep allured and captured his eyes.

In winter he spent his days by the fireside, pondering the wailing of the winds and lamentation of the elements, meditating upon the phenomena of the seasons, and looking through the window toward the snow-laden valleys and leafless trees, symbolizing a multitude of suffering people left helpless in the jaws of biting frost and strong wind.

During the long winter nights he sat up until his parents retired, whereupon he opened a rough wooden closet, brought out his New Testament, and read it secretly under the dim light of a flickering lamp. The priests objected to the reading of the Good Book, and John exercised great caution during these fascinating moments of study. The fathers warned the simple-hearted people against its use, and threatened them with excommunication from the church if discovered possessing it.

Thus John spent his youth between the beautiful earth of God and the New Testament, full of light and truth. John was a youth of silence and contemplation; he listened to his parents' conversations and never spoke a word nor asked a question. When sitting with his contemporaries, he gazed steadily at the horizon, and his thoughts were as distant as his eyes. After each visit to the church he returned home with a depressed spirit, for the teachings of the priests were different from the precepts he found in the Gospel, and the life of the faithful was not the beautiful life of which Christ spoke.

\*     \*     \*     \*     \*

Spring came and the snow melted in the fields and valleys. The snow upon the mountain tops was thawing gradually and forming many streamlets in the winding paths leading into the valleys, combining into a torrent whose roaring bespoke the awakening of Nature. The almond and apple trees were in full bloom; the willow and poplar trees were sprouting with buds, and Nature had spread her happy and colourful garments over the countryside.

John, tired of spending his days by the fireside, and knowing that his oxen were longing for the pastures, released his animals from the sheds and led them to the fields, concealing his New Testament under his cloak for fear of detection. He reached a beautiful arbor adjacent to some fields belonging to the St. Elija Monastery * which stood majestically upon a nearby hill. As the oxen commenced grazing, John leaned upon a rock and began to read his New Testament and meditate the sadness of the children of God on earth, and the beauty of the Kingdom of Heaven.

It was the last day of Lent, and the villagers who abstained from eating meat were impatiently awaiting the coming of Easter. John, like the rest of the poor fellahin, never distinguished Lent from any other day of the year, for his whole life was an extended Lent, and his food never exceeded the simple bread, kneaded with the pain of his heart, or the fruits, purchased with the blood of his body. The only nourishment craved by John during Lent was that spiritual food—the heavenly bread that brought into his heart sad thoughts of the tragedy of the Son of Man and the end of His life on earth.

The birds were singing and hovering about him, and large flocks of doves circled in the sky,

* A rich abbey in North Lebanon with vast lands, occupied by scores of monks called Alepoans. (Editor's note.)

while the flowers swayed with the breeze as if exhilarated by the brilliant sunshine.

John busied himself absorbing the Book, and between these intense, light-giving sessions, he watched the domes of the churches in the nearby villages and listened to the rhythmic toll of the bells. Occasionally he would close his eyes and fly on the wings of dreams to Old Jerusalem, following Christ's steps and asking the people of the city about the Nazarene, whereupon he would receive the answer, "Here He cured the paralyzed and restored to the blind their sight; and there they braided for Him a wreath of thorns and placed it upon His head; from that portico He spoke to the multitude with beautiful parables; in that palace they tied Him to the marble columns and scourged Him; on this road He forgave the adulteress her sins, and upon that spot He fell under the weight of His Cross."

\*    \*    \*    \*    \*

One hour passed, and John was suffering physically with God and glorifying with Him in spirit.

149

Noon quickly came, and the oxen were beyond the reach of John's sight. He looked in every direction but could not see them, and as he reached the trail that led to the adjacent fields, he saw a man at a distance, standing amidst the orchards. As he approached and saw that the man was one of the Monastery's monks, he greeted him, bowed reverently, and asked him if he had seen the oxen. The monk appeared to be restraining anger, and he said, "Yes, I saw them. Follow me and I will show them to you." As they reached the Monastery, John found his oxen tied with ropes in a shed. One of the monks was acting as a watchman over them, and each time an animal moved, he struck the ox across the back with a heavy club. John made a frantic attempt to unbind the helpless animals, but the monk took hold of his cloak and withheld him. At the same time he turned toward the Monastery and shouted, saying, "Here is the criminal shepherd! I have found him!" The priests and monks, preceded by the head priest, hurried to the scene and encircled John, who was bewildered, and felt like a captive. "I have done nothing to merit the treatment of a criminal," said John to the head priest. And the leader replied angrily, "Your oxen have ruined our plantation and destroyed our vineyards. Since you are responsible for the damage we will not give up your oxen until you adjust our loss."

John protested, "I am poor and have no money. Please release my oxen and I pledge my honour that I will never again bring them to these lands." The head priest took a step forward, raised his hand toward heaven, and said, "God has appointed us to be the protectors over this vast land of St. Elija, and it is our sacred duty to guard it with all of our might, for this land is holy, and, like fire, it will burn any who trespass upon it. If you refuse to account for your crime against God, the grass that your oxen have eaten will surely turn into poison and destroy them!"

The head priest started to depart, but John touched his robe and humbly begged, "I appeal to you in the name of Jesus and all the saints, to let me and my animals free. Be kind to me, for I am poor, and the coffers of the Monastery are bursting with silver and gold. Have mercy upon my poor and aged parents, whose lives depend on me. God will forgive me if I have harmed you." The head priest looked at him with severity, and said, "Poor or rich, the Monastery cannot forgive you your debts; three denars will free your oxen." John pleaded, "I do not possess a single coin; have mercy on a poor grazier, Father." And the head priest retorted, "Then you must sell a part of your possessions and bring three denars, for it is better to enter the Kingdom of Heaven without property than to bring the wrath of St. Elija upon you and descend to hell." The other monks nodded their accord.

After a short silence, John's face brightened and his eyes shone as if fear and servility had deserted his heart. With his head high, he looked at the head priest and addressed him boldly, saying, "Do the weak poor have to sell their pitiful belongings, the source of their life's bread, in order to add more gold to the Monastery's wealth? Is it just that the poor should be oppressed and made poorer in order that St. Elija may forgive the oxen their innocent wrongs?" The head priest raised his eyes to heaven and intoned, "It is written in the Book of God that he who has plenty shall be given more, and he who has not shall be taken from."

When John heard these words he became furious, and like a soldier who draws his sword in the face of the enemy, he drew the New Testament from his pocket and shouted out, "This is how you twist the teachings of Christ, you hypocrite! And thus do you pervert the most sacred heritage of life in order to spread your evils. . . . Woe to you when the Son of Man comes again and destroys your Monastery and throws its debris in the valley, and burns your shrine and altars into ashes. . . . Woe to you when the wrath of the Nazarene descends upon you and throws you into the depths of the abyss. . . . Woe to you, worshippers of the idols of greed, who hide the ugliness of hatred under your black garments. . . . Woe to you, foes of Jesus, who move your lips with prayers while your hearts are laden with lusts. . . . Woe to you who kneel before the altar

153

in body while your spirits are revolting against God! You are polluted with your own sin of punishing me for approaching your land, paid for by me and my ancestors. You ridiculed me when I asked for mercy in the name of Christ. Take this Book and show your smiling monks where the Son of God ever refused to forgive. . . . Read this heavenly tragedy and tell them where He spoke not of mercy and of kindness, be it in the Sermon of the Mount, or in the temple. Did He not forgive the adulteress her sins? Did He not part his hands upon the Cross to embrace humanity? Look upon our wretched homes, where the sick suffer upon their hard beds. . . . Look behind the prison bars, where the innocent man is victim of oppression and injustice. . . . Look upon the beggars, stretching forth their hands for alms, humiliated in heart and broken in body. . . . Think upon your slaving followers, who are suffering the pangs of hunger while you are living a life of luxury and indifference, and enjoying the fruits of the fields and the wine of the vineyards. You have never visited a sufferer nor consoled the down-hearted nor fed ʋie hungry; neither have you sheltered the wayfarer nor offered sympathy to the lame. Yet you are not satisfied with what you have pilfered from our fathers, but still stretch your hands like vipers' heads, grasping by threats of hell what little a widow has saved through body-breaking toil, or a miserable fellah has stored away to keep his children alive!"

John took a deep breath, then calmed his voice and quietly added, "You are numerous, and I am alone—you may do unto me what you wish; the wolves prey upon the lamb in the darkness of the night, but the blood stains remain upon the stones in the valley until the dawn comes, and the sun reveals the crime to all."

There was a magic power in John's talk that arrested their attention and injected a defensive anger into the monks' hearts. They were shaking with fury and waiting only for their superior's order to fall upon John and bring him to submission. The brief silence was like the heavy quiet of the tempest, after laying waste the gardens. The head priest then commanded the monks, saying, "Bind this criminal and take the Book from him and drag him into a dark cell, for he who blasphemes the holy representatives of God will never be forgiven on this earth, neither in Eternity." The Monks leaped upon John and led him manacled into a narrow prison and barred him there.

The courage shown by John could not be perceived or understood by one who partakes of the submission or the deceit or the tyranny of this enslaved country, called by the Orientals "The Bride of Syria," and "The Pearl of the Sultan's Crown." And in his cell, John thought of the needless misery brought upon his countrymen by the grip of the things he had just learned. He smiled with a sad sympathy and his smile was mingled with suffering and bitterness; the kind that cuts its way through the depths of the heart; the kind that sets the soul to a choking futility; the kind which, if left unsupported, ascends to the eyes and falls down helplessly.

John then stood proudly, and looked through the window-slit facing the sunlit valley. He felt as if a spiritual joy were embracing his soul and a sweet tranquility possessing his heart. They had imprisoned his body, but his spirit was sailing freely with the breeze amidst the knolls and prairies. His love for Jesus never changed, and the torturing hands could not remove his heart's ease, for persecution cannot harm him who stands by Truth. Did not Socrates fall proudly a victim in body? Was not Paul stoned for the sake of the Truth? It is our inner selves that hurt us when we disobey it, and it kills us when we betray it.

*    *    *    *    *

John's parents were informed of his imprisonment and the confiscation of the oxen. His old mother came to the Monastery leaning heavily over her walking stick and she prostrated herself before the head priest, kissing his feet and begging him for mercy upon her only son. The head priest raised his head reverently toward heaven and said, "We will forgive your son for his madness, but St. Elija will not forgive any who trespass upon his land." After gazing at him with tearful eyes, the old lady took a silver locket from her neck and handed it to the head priest, saying, "This is my most precious possession, given to me as a wedding gift by my mother. . . . Will you accept it as atonement for my son's sin?"

The head priest took the locket and placed it in his pocket, whereupon he looked at John's ancient mother who was kissing his hands and expressing to him her thanks and gratitude, and he said, "Woe to this sinful age! You twist the saying of the Good Book and cause the children to eat the sour, and the parents' teeth sit on edge; go now, good woman, and pray to God for your mad son and ask Him to restore his mind."

John left the prison, and walked quietly by the side of his mother, driving the oxen before him. When they reached their wretched hovel, he led the animals into their mangers and sat silently by the window, meditating the sunset. In a few moments he heard his father whispering to his mother, saying, "Sara, many times have I told you that John was mad, and you disbelieved. Now you will agree, after what you have seen, for the head priest has spoken to you today the very words I spoke to you in past years." John continued looking toward the distant horizon, watching the sun descend.

*     *     *     *     *

Easter arrived, and at that time the construction of a new church in the town of Bsherri had just been completed. This magnificent place of worship was like a prince's palace standing amidst the huts of poor subjects. The people were scurrying through the many preparations to receive a prelate who was assigned to officiate at the religious ceremonies inaugurating the new temple. The multitudes stood in rows over the roads waiting for His Grace's arrival. The chanting of the priests in unison with cymbal sounds and the hymns of the throngs filled the sky.

The prelate finally arrived, riding a magnificent horse harnessed with a gold-studded saddle, and as he dismounted, the priests and political leaders met him with the most beautiful of welcoming speeches. He was escorted to the new altar, where he clothed himself in ecclesiastical raiment, decorated with gold threads and encrusted with sparkling gems; he wore the golden crown, and walked in a procession around the altar, carrying his jewelled staff. He was followed by the priests and the carriers of tapers and incense burners.

At that hour, John stood amongst the fellahin at the portico, contemplating the scene with bitter sighs and sorrowful eyes, for it pained him to observe the expensive robes, and precious crown, and staff, and vases and other objects of needless extravagance, while the poor fellahin who came from the surrounding villages to celebrate the occasion were suffering the gnawing pangs of poverty. Their tattered swaddles and sorrowful faces bespoke their miserable plight.

The rich dignitaries, decorated with badges and ribbons, stood aloof praying loudly, while the suffering villagers, in the rear of the scene, beat their bosoms in sincere prayer that came from the depths of their broken hearts.

The authority of those dignitaries and leaders

was like the ever-green leaves of the poplar trees, and the life of those fellahin was like a boat whose pilot had met his destiny and whose rudder had been lost and whose sails had been torn by the strong wind and left at the mercy of the furious depths and the raging tempest.

Tyranny and blind submission . . . which one of these gave birth to the other? Is tyranny a strong tree that grows not in the low earth, or is it submission, which is like a deserted field where naught but thorns can grow? Such thoughts and contemplations prayed on John's mind while the ceremonies were taking place; he braced his arms about his chest for fear his bosom would burst with agony over the people's plight in this tragedy of opposites.

He gazed upon the withering creatures of severe humanity, whose hearts were dry and whose seeds were now seeking shelter in the bosom of the earth, as destitute pilgrims seek rebirth in a new realm.

When the pageantry came to an end and the multitude was preparing to disperse, John felt that a compelling power was urging him to speak in behalf of the oppressed poor. He proceeded to an extreme end of the square, raised his hands toward the sky, and as the throngs gathered about, he opened his lips and said, "O Jesus, Who art sitting in the heart of the circle of light, give heed! Look upon this earth from behind the blue dome and see how the thorns have choked the flowers which Thy truth hast planted.

"Oh Good Shepherd, the wolves have preyed upon the weak lamb which Thou hast carried in Thy arms. Thy pure blood has been drawn into the depths of the earth which Thy feet have made sacred. This good earth has been made by Thine enemies into an arena where the strong crushes the weak. The cry of the miserable and the lamentation of the helpless can no longer be heard by those sitting upon the thrones, preaching Thy word. The lambs which Thou hast sent to this earth are now wolves who eat the one which Thou hast carried and blessed.

"The word of light which sprang forth from Thy heart has vanished from the scripture and is replaced with an empty and terrible uproar that frightens the spirit.

"Oh Jesus, they have built these churches for the sake of their own glory, and embellished them with silk and melted gold. . . . They left the bodies of Thy chosen poor wrapped in tattered raiment in the cold night. . . . They filled the sky with the smoke of burning candles and incense and left the bodies of Thy faithful worshippers empty of bread. . . . They raised their voices with hymns of praise, but deafened themselves to the cry and moan of the widows and orphans.

"Come again, Oh Living Jesus, and drive the vendors of Thy faith from Thy sacred temple, for they have turned it into a dark cave where vipers of hypocrisy and falsehood crawl and abound."

John's words, strong and sincere, brought murmurs of approval, and the approach of the dignitaries quelled him not. With added courage, strengthened by memories of his earlier experience, he continued, "Come, Oh Jesus, and render accounts with those Caesars who usurped from the weak what is the weak's and from God what is God's. The grapevine which Thou has planted with Thy right hand has been eaten by worms of greed and its bunches have been trampled down. Thy sons of peace are dividing amongst themselves and fighting one with another, leaving poor souls as victims in the wintry field. Before Thy altar, they raise their voices with prayers, saying, 'Glory to God in the highest, and on earth peace, good will toward men.' Will our Father in heaven be glorified when His name is uttered by empty hearts and sinful lips and false tongues? Will peace be on earth while the sons of misery are slaving in the fields to feed the strong and fill the stomachs of the tyrants? Will ever peace come and save them from the clutches of destitution?

"What is peace? Is it in the eyes of those infants, nursing upon the dry breasts of their hungry mothers in cold huts? Or is it in the wretched hovels of the hungry who sleep upon hard beds and crave for one bite of the food which the priests and monks feed to their fat pigs?

"What is joy, Oh Beautiful Jesus? Is it manifest

when the Emir buys the strong arms of men and the honour of women for threats of death or for a few pieces of silver? Or is it found in submission, and slaving of body and spirit to those who dazzle our eyes with their glittering badges and golden diadems? Upon each complaint to Thy peace makers, they reward us with their soldiers, armed with swords and spears to step upon our women and children and steal our blood.

"Oh Jesus, full of love and mercy, stretch forth Thy strong arms and protect us from those thieves or send welcome Death to deliver us and lead us to the graves where we can rest peacefully under the watchful care of Thy Cross; there we shall wait for Thy return. Oh Mighty Jesus, this life is naught but a dark cell of enslavement. . . . It is a playing ground of horrible ghosts, and it is a pit alive with spectres of death. Our days are but sharp swords concealed under the ragged quilts of our beds in the fearful darkness of the night. At dawn, these weapons rise above our heads as demons, pointing out to us our whip-driven slavery in the fields.

"Oh Jesus, have mercy upon the oppressed poor who came today to commemorate Thy Resurrection. . . . Pity them, for they are miserable and weak."

John's talk appealed to one group and displeased another. "He is telling the truth, and speaking in our behalf before heaven," one remarked. And another one said, "He is bewitched, for he speaks in the name of an evil spirit." And a third commented, "We have never heard such infamous talk, not even from our fathers! We must bring it to an end!" And a fourth one said, whispering into the next man's ears, "I felt a new spirit in me when I heard him talking." The next man added, "But the priests know our needs more so than he does; it is a sin to doubt them." As the voices grew from every direction like the roar of the sea, one of the priests approached, placed John in restraint and turned him immediately to the law, whereupon he was taken to the Governor's palace for trial.

Upon his interrogation, John uttered not a single word, for he knew that the Nazarene resorted to silence before His persecutors. The governor ordered John to be placed in a prison, where he slept peacefully and heart-cleansed that night, leaning his head on the rock wall of the dungeon.

The next day John's father came and testified before the Governor that his son was mad, and added, sadly, "Many times have I heard him talking to himself and speaking of many strange things that none could see or understand. Many times did he sit talking in the silence of the night, using vague words. I heard him calling the ghosts with a voice like that of a sorcerer. You may ask the neighbours who talked to him and found beyond doubt that he was insane. He never answered when one spoke to him, and when he spoke, he uttered cryptic words and phrases unknown to the listener and out of the subject. His mother knows him well. Many times she saw him gazing at the distant horizon with glazed eyes and speaking with passion, like a small child, about the brooks and the flowers and the stars. Ask the monks whose teachings he ridiculed and criticized during their sacred Lent. He is insane,

Your Excellency, but he is very kind to me and to his mother; he does much to help us in our old age, and he works with diligence to keep us fed and warm and alive. Pity him, and have mercy on us."

The Governor released John, and the news of his madness spread throughout the village. And when the people spoke of John they mentioned his name with humour and ridicule, and the maidens looked upon him with sorrowful eyes and said, "Heaven has its strange purpose in man. . . . God united beauty and insanity in this youth, and joined the kind brightness of his eyes with the darkness of his unseen self."

*     *     *     *     *

In the midst of God's fields and prairies, and by the side of the knolls, carpeted with green grass and beautiful flowers, the ghost of John, alone and restless, watches the oxen grazing peacefully, undisturbed by man's hardships. With tearful eyes he looks toward the scattered villages on both sides of the valley and repeats with deep sighs, "You are numerous and I am alone; the wolves prey upon the lambs in the darkness of the night, but the blood stains remain upon the stones in the valley until the dawn comes, and the sun reveals the crime to all."

# The Enchanting Houri

# The Enchanting Houri

WHERE are you leading me, Oh Enchanting
Houri, and how long shall I follow you
Upon this hispid road, planted with
Thorns? How long shall our souls ascend
And descend painfully on this twisting
And rocky path?

Like a child following his mother I am
Following you, holding the extreme end
Of your garment, forgetting my dreams
And staring at your beauty, blinding
My eyes under your spell to the
Procession of spectres hovering above
Me, and attracted to you by an inner
Force within me which I cannot deny.

Halt for a moment and let me see your
Countenance; and look upon me for a

Moment; perhaps I will learn your
Heart's secrets through your strange
Eyes. Stop and rest, for I am weary,
And my soul is trembling with fear
Upon this horrible trail. Halt, for
We have reached that terrible crossroad
Where Death embraces Life.

*     *     *     *     *

Oh Houri, listen to me! I was as free
As the birds, probing the valleys and
The forests, and flying in the spacious
Sky. At eventide I rested upon the
Branches of the trees, meditating the
Temples and palaces in the City of the
Colorful Clouds which the Sun builds
In the morning and destroys before
Twilight.

I was like a thought, walking alone
And at peace to the East and West of
The Universe, rejoicing with the
Beauty and joy of Life, and inquiring

174

Into the magnificent mystery of
Existence.

I was like a dream, stealing out under
The friendly wings of the night,
Entering through the closed windows
Into the maidens' chambers, frolicking
And awakening their hopes. . . . Then I
Sat by the youths and agitated their
Desires. . . . Then I probed the elders'
Quarters and penetrated their thoughts
Of serene contentment.

Then you captured my fancy, and since
That hypnotic moment I felt like a
Prisoner dragging his shackles and
Impelled into an unknown place. . . .
I became intoxicated with your sweet
Wine that has stolen my will, and I
Now find my lips kissing the hand
That strikes me sharply. Can you
Not see with your soul's eye the
Crushing of my heart? Halt for a

Moment; I am regaining my strength
And untying my weary feet from the
Heavy chains. I have crushed the
Cup from which I have drunk your
Tasty venom. . . . But now I am in
A strange land, and bewildered;
Which road shall I follow?

My freedom has been restored; will
You now accept me as a willing
Companion, who looks at the Sun
With glazed eyes and grasps the
Fire with untrembling fingers?

I have unbound my wings and I am
Ready to ascend; will you accompany
A youth who spends his days roaming
The mountains like the lone eagle, and
Wastes his nights wandering in the
Deserts like the restless lion?

Will you content yourself with the
Affection of one who looks upon Love

176

As but an entertainer, and declines
To accept her as his master?

Will you accept a heart that loves,
But never yields? And burns, but
Never melts? Will you be at ease
With a soul that quivers before the
Tempest, but never surrenders to it?
Will you accept one as a companion
Who makes not slaves, nor will become
One? Will you own me but not possess
Me, by taking my body and not my heart?

Then here is my hand—grasp it with
Your beautiful hand; and here is my
Body—embrace it with your loving
Arms; and here are my lips—bestow
Upon them a deep and dizzying kiss.

# Behind the Garment

# Behind the Garment

Rachel woke at midnight and gazed intently at something invisible in the sky of her chamber. She heard a voice more soothing than the whispers of Life, and more dismal than the moaning call of the abyss, and softer than the rustling of white wings, and deeper than the message of the waves. . . . It vibrated with hope and with futility, with joy and with misery, and with affection for life, yet with desire for death. Then Rachel closed her eyes and sighed deeply, and gasped, saying, "Dawn has reached the extreme end of the valley; we should go toward the sun and meet him." Her lips were parted, resembling and echoing a deep wound in the soul.

At that moment the priest approached her bed and felt her hand, but found it as cold as the snow; and when he grimly placed his fingers upon her heart, he determined that it was as immobile as the ages, and as silent as the secret of his heart.

The reverend father bowed his head in deep despair. His lips quivered as if wanting to utter a divine word, repeated by the phantoms of the night in the distant and deserted valleys.

After crossing her arms upon her bosom, the priest looked toward a man sitting in an obscured corner of the room, and with a kind and merciful voice he said, "Your beloved has reached the great circle of light. Come, my brother, let us kneel and pray."

The sorrowful husband lifted his head; his eyes stared, gazing at the unseen, and his expression then changed as if he saw understanding in the ghost of an unknown God. He gathered the remnants of himself and walked reverently toward the bed of his wife, and knelt by the side of the clergyman who was praying and lamenting and making the sign of the cross.

Placing his hand upon the shoulder of the grief-stricken husband, the Father said quietly, "Go to the adjoining room, brother, for you are in great need of rest."

He rose obediently, walked to the room and threw his fatigued body upon a narrow bed, and in a few moments he was sailing in the world of sleep like a little child taking refuge in the merciful arms of his loving mother.

* * * * *

The priest remained standing like a statue in the center of the room, and a strange conflict gripped him. And he looked with tearful eyes first at the cold body of the young woman and then through the parted curtain at her husband, who had surrendered himself to the allure of slumber. An hour, longer than an age and more terrible than Death, had already passed, and the priest was still standing between two parted souls. One was dreaming as a field dreams of the coming Spring after the tragedy of Winter, and the other was resting eternally.

Then the priest came close to the body of the young woman and knelt as if worshipping before the altar; he held her cold hand and placed it against his trembling lips, and looked at her face that was adorned with the soft veil of Death. His voice was at the same time calm as the night and deep as the chasm and faltering as with the hopes of man. And in voice he wept, "Oh Rachel, bride of my soul, hear me! At last I am able to talk! Death has opened my lips so that I can now reveal to you a secret deeper than Life itself. Pain has unpinioned my tongue and I can disclose to you my suffering, more painful than pain. Listen to the cry of my soul, Oh Pure Spirit, hovering between the earth and the firmament. Give heed to the youth who waited for you to come from the field, gazing upon you from behind the trees, in fear of your beauty. Hear the priest, who is serving God, calling to you unashamed, after you have reached the City of God. I have proved the strength of my love by concealing it!"

Having thus opened his soul, the Father leaned over and printed three long, warm, and mute kisses upon her forehead, eyes and throat, pouring forth all his heart's secret of love and pain,

184

and the anguish of the years. Then he suddenly withdrew to the dark corner and dropped in agony upon the floor, shaking like an Autumn leaf, as if the touch of her cold face had awakened within him the spirit to repent; whereupon he composed himself and knelt, hiding has face with his cupped hands, and he whispered softly, "God. . . . Forgive my sin; forgive my weakness, Oh Lord. I could no longer resist disclosing tnat which You knew. Seven years have I kept the deep secrets hidden in my heart from the spoken word, until Death came and tore them from me. Help me, Oh God, to hide this terrible and beautiful memory which brings sweetness from life and bitterness from You. Forgive me, My Lord, and forgive my weakness."

Without looking at the young woman's corpse, he continued suffering and lamenting until Dawn came and dropped a rosy veil upon those two still images, revealing the conflict of Love and Religion to one man; the peace of Life and Death to the other.

# Dead Are My People

# Dead Are My People

(*Written in exile during the famine in Syria*)
"WORLD WAR I"

Gone are my people, but I exist yet,
Lamenting them in my solitude. . . .
Dead are my friends, and in their
Death my life is naught but great
Disaster.

The knolls of my country are submerged
By tears and blood, for my people and
My beloved are gone, and I am here
Living as I did when my people and my
Beloved were enjoying life and the
Bounty of life, and when the hills of
My country were blessed and engulfed
By the light of the sun.

My people died from hunger, and he who
Did not perish from starvation was

Butchered with the sword; and I am
Here in this distant land, roaming
Amongst a joyful people who sleep
Upon soft beds, and smile at the days
While the days smile upon them.

My people died a painful and shameful
Death, and here am I living in plenty
And in peace. . . . This is deep tragedy
Ever-enacted upon the stage of my
Heart; few would care to witness this
Drama, for my people are as birds with
Broken wings, left behind by the flock.

If I were hungry and living amid my
Famished people, and persecuted among
My oppressed countrymen, the burden
Of the black days would be lighter
Upon my restless dreams, and the
Obscurity of the night would be less
Dark before my hollow eyes and my
Crying heart and my wounded soul.
For he who shares with his people

Their sorrow and agony will feel a
Supreme comfort created only by
Suffering in sacrifice. And he will
Be at peace with himself when he dies
Innocent with his fellow innocents.

But I am not living with my hungry
And persecuted people who are walking
In the procession of death toward
Martyrdom. . . . I am here beyond the
Broad seas living in the shadow of
Tranquility, and in the sunshine of
Peace. . . . I am afar from the pitiful
Arena and the distressed, and cannot
Be proud of aught, not even of my own
Tears.

What can an exiled son do for his
Starving people, and of what value
Unto them is the lamentation of an
Absent poet?

Were I an ear of corn grown in the earth
Of my country, the hungry child would

Pluck me and remove with my kernels
The hand of Death from his soul. Were
I a ripe fruit in the gardens of my
Country, the starving woman would
Gather me and sustain life. Were I
A bird flying in the sky of my country,
My hungry brother would hunt me and
Remove with the flesh of my body the
Shadow of the grave from his body.
But alas! I am not an ear of corn
Grown in the plains of Syria, nor a
Ripe fruit in the valleys of Lebanon;
This is my disaster, and this is my
Mute calamity which brings humiliation
Before my soul and before the phantoms
Of the night. . . .This is the painful
Tragedy which tightens my tongue and
Pinions my arms and arrests me usurped
Of power and of will and of action.
This is the curse burned upon my
Forehead before God and man.

*     *     *     *     *

And oftentime they say unto me,
"The disaster of your country is
But naught to the calamity of the
World, and the tears and blood shed
By your people are as nothing to
The rivers of blood and tears
Pouring each day and night in the
Valleys and plains of the earth. . . ."


Yes, but the death of my people is
A silent accusation; it is a crime
Conceived by the heads of the unseen
Serpents. . . . It is a songless and
Sceneless tragedy. . . . And if my
People had attacked the despots
And oppressors and died as rebels,
I would have said, "Dying for
Freedom is nobler than living in
The shadow of weak submission, for
He who embraces death with the sword
Of Truth in his hand will eternalize
With the Eternity of Truth, for Life

Is weaker than Death and Death is
Weaker than Truth.

If my nation had partaken in the war
Of all nations and had died in the
Field of battle, I would say that
The raging tempest had broken with
Its might the green branches; and
Strong death under the canopy of
The tempest is nobler than slow
Perishment in the arms of senility.
But there was no rescue from the
Closing jaws. . . . My people dropped
And wept with the crying angels.

If an earthquake had torn my
Country asunder and the earth had
Engulfed my people into its bosom,
I would have said, "A great and
Mysterious law has been moved by
The will of divine force, and it
Would be pure madness if we frail
Mortals endeavoured to probe its

194

Deep secrets. . . ."
But my people did not die as rebels;
They were not killed in the field
Of battle; nor did the earthquake
Shatter my country and subdue them.
Death was their only rescuer, and
Starvation their only spoils.

\*     \*     \*     \*     \*

My people died on the cross. . . .
They died while their hands
Stretched toward the East and West,
While the remnants of their eyes
Stared at the blackness of the
Firmament. . . . They died silently,
For humanity had closed its ears
To their cry. They died because
They did not befriend their enemy.
They died because they loved their
Neighbours. They died because
They placed trust in all humanity.
They died because they did not
Oppress the oppressors. They died

Because they were the crushed
Flowers, and not the crushing feet.
They died because they were peace
Makers. They perished from hunger
In a land rich with milk and honey.
They died because the monsters of
Hell arose and destroyed all that
Their fields grew, and devoured the
Last provisions in their bins. . . .
They died because the vipers and
Sons of vipers spat out poison into
The space where the Holy Cedars and
The roses and the jasmine breathe
Their fragrance.

My people and your people, my Syrian
Brother, are dead. . . . What can be
Done for those who are dying? Our
Lamentations will not satisfy their
Hunger, and our tears will not quench
Their thirst; what can we do to save
Them from between the iron paws of
Hunger? My brother, the kindness

Which compels you to give a part of
Your life to any human who is in the
Shadow of losing his life is the only
Virtue which makes you worthy of the
Light of day and the peace of the
Night. . . . Remember, my brother,
That the coin which you drop into
The withered hand stretching toward
You is the only golden chain that
Binds your rich heart to the
Loving heart of God. . . .

# The Ambitious Violet

# The Ambitious Violet

THERE was a beautiful and fragrant violet who lived placidly amongst her friends, and swayed happily amidst the other flowers in a solitary garden. One morning, as her crown was embellished with beads of dew, she lifted her head and looked about; she saw a tall and handsome rose standing proudly and reaching high into space, like a burning torch upon an emerald lamp.

The violet opened her blue lips and said, "What an unfortunate am I among these flowers, and how humble is the position I occupy in their presence! Nature has fashioned me to be short and poor. . . . I live very close to the earth and I cannot raise my head toward the blue sky, or turn my face to the sun, as the roses do."

And the rose heard her neighbour's words; she laughed and commented, "How strange is your talk! You are fortunate, and yet you cannot understand your fortune. Nature has bestowed upon you fragrance and beauty which she did not grant to any other. . . . Cast aside your thoughts and be contented, and remember that he who humbles himself will be exalted, and he who exalts himself will be crushed."

The violet answered, "You are consoling me because you have that which I crave. . . . You seek to embitter me with the meaning that you are great. . . . How painful is the preaching of the fortunate to the heart of the miserable! And how severe is the strong when he stands as advisor among the weak!"

* * * * *

And Nature heard the conversation of the violet and the rose; she approached and said, "What has happened to you, my daughter violet? You have been humble and sweet in all your deeds and words. Has greed entered your heart and numbed your senses?" In a pleading voice, the violet answered her, saying, "Oh great and merciful mother, full of love and sympathy, I beg you, with all my heart and soul, to grant my request and allow me to be a rose for one day."

And Nature responded, "You know not what you are seeking; you are unaware of the concealed disaster behind your blind ambition. If you were a rose you would be sorry, and repentance would avail you but naught." The violet insisted, "Change me into a tall rose, for I wish to lift my head high with pride; and regardless of my fate, it will be my own doing." Nature yielded, saying, "Oh ignorant and rebellious violet, I will grant your request. But if calamity befalls you, your complaint must be to yourself."

And Nature stretched forth her mysterious and magic fingers and touched the roots of the violet, who immediately turned into a tall rose, rising above all other flowers in the garden.

At eventide the sky became thick with black clouds, and the raging elements disturbed the silence of existence with thunder, and commenced to attack the garden, sending forth a great rain and strong winds. The tempest tore the branches and uprooted the plants and broke the stems of the tall flowers, sparing only the little ones who grew close to the friendly earth. That solitary garden suffered greatly from the belligerent skies, and when the storm calmed and the sky cleared, all the flowers were laid waste and none of them had escaped the wrath of Nature except the clan of small violets, hiding by the wall of the garden.

*　　*　　*　　*　　*

Having lifted her head and viewed the tragedy of the flowers and trees, one of the violet maidens smiled happily and called to her companions, saying, "See what the tempest has done to the haughty flowers!" Another violet said, "We are small, and live close to the earth, but we are safe from the wrath of the skies." And a third one added, "Because we are poor in height the tempest is unable to subdue us."

At that moment the queen of violets saw by her side the converted violet, hurled to earth by the storm and distorted upon the wet grass like a limp soldier in a battle field. The queen of the violets lifted her head and called to her family, saying, "Look, my daughters, and meditate upon that which Greed has done to the violet who became a proud rose for one hour. Let the memory of this scene be a reminder of your good fortune."

And the dying rose moved and gathered the remnants of her strength, and quietly said, "You are contented and meek dullards; I have never feared the tempest. Yesterday I, too, was satisfied and contented with Life, but Contentment has acted as a barrier between my existence and the tempest of Life, confining me to a sickly and sluggish peace and tranquility of mind. I could have lived the same life you are living now by clinging with fear to the earth. . . . I could have waited for winter to shroud me with snow and deliver me to Death, who will surely claim all violets. . . . I am happy now because I have probed outside my little world into the mystery of the Universe . . . something which you have not yet done. I could have overlooked Greed, whose nature is higher than mine, but as I hearkened to the silence of the night, I heard the heavenly world talking to this earthly world, saying,

'Ambition beyond existence is the essential purpose of our being.' At that moment my spirit revolted and my heart longed for a position higher than my limited existence. I realized that the abyss cannot hear the song of the stars, and at that moment I commenced fighting against my smallness and craving for that which did not belong to me, until my rebelliousness turned into a great power, and my longing into a creating will. . . . Nature, who is the great object of our deeper dreams, granted my request and changed me into a rose with her magic fingers."

The rose became silent for a moment, and in a weakening voice, mingled with pride and achievement, she said, "I have lived one hour as a proud rose; I have existed for a time like a queen; I have looked at the Universe from behind the eyes of the rose; I have heard the whisper of the firmament through the ears of the rose and touched the folds of Light's garment with rose petals. Is there any here who can claim such honour?" Having thus spoken, she lowered her head, and with a choking voice she gasped, "I shall die now, for my soul has attained its goal. I have finally extended my knowledge to a world beyond the narrow cavern of my birth. This is the design of Life. . . . This is the secret of Existence." Then the rose quivered, slowly folded her petals, and breathed her last with a heavenly smile upon her lips . . . a smile of fulfillment of hope and purpose in Life . . . a smile of victory . . . a God's smile.

# The Crucified

# The Crucified

## (*Written on Good Friday*)

Today, and on this same day of each year, man is startled from his deep slumber and stands before the phantoms of the Ages, looking with tearful eyes toward Mount Calvary to witness Jesus the Nazarene nailed on the Cross. . . . But when the day is over and eventide comes, human kinds return and kneel praying before the idols, erected upon every hilltop, every prairie, and every barter of wheat.

Today, the Christian souls ride on the wing of memories and fly to Jerusalem. There they will stand in throngs, beating upon their bosoms, and staring at Him, crowned with a wreath of thorns, stretching His arms before heaven, and looking from behind the veil of Death into the depths of Life. . . .

But when the curtain of night drops over the

stage of the day and the brief drama is concluded, the Christians will go back in groups and lie down in the shadow of oblivion between the quilts of ignorance and slothfulness.

On this one day of each year, the philosophers leave their dark caves, and the thinkers their cold cells, and the poets their imaginary arbors, and all stand reverently upon that silent mountain, listening to the voice of a young man saying of His killers, "Oh Father, forgive them, for they know not what they are doing."

But as dark silence chokes the voices of the light, the philosophers and the thinkers and the poets return to their narrow crevices and shroud their souls with meaningless pages of parchment.

The women who busy themselves in the splendour of Life will bestir themselves today from their cushions to see the sorrowful woman standing before the Cross like a tender sapling before the raging tempest; and when they approach near to her, they will hear a deep moaning and a painful grief.

The young men and women who are racing

with the torrent of modern civilization will halt today for a moment, and look backward to see the young Magdalen washing with her tears the blood stains from the feet of a Holy Man suspended between Heaven and Earth; and when their shallow eyes weary of the scene they will depart and soon laugh.

On this day of each year, Humanity wakes with the awakening of the Spring, and stands crying below the suffering Nazarene; then she closes her eyes and surrenders herself to a deep slumber. But Spring will remain awake, smiling and progressing until merged into Summer, dressed in scented golden raiment. Humanity is a mourner who enjoys lamenting the memories and heroes of the Ages. . . . If Humanity were possessed of understanding, there would be rejoicing over their glory. Humanity is like a child standing in glee by a wounded beast. Humanity laughs before the strengthening torrent which carries into oblivion the dry branches of the trees, and sweeps away with determination all things not fastened to strength.

Humanity looks upon Jesus the Nazarene as a poor-born Who suffered misery and humiliation with all of the weak. And He is pitied, for Humanity believes He was crucified painfully. . . . And all that Humanity offers to Him is crying and wailing and lamentation. For centuries Humanity has been worshipping weakness in the person of the Saviour.

The Nazarene was not weak! He was strong and is strong! But the people refuse to heed the true meaning of strength.

Jesus never lived a life of fear, nor did He die suffering or complaining. . . . He lived as a leader; He was crucified as a crusader; He died with a heroism that frightened His killers and tormentors.

Jesus was not a bird with broken wings; He was a raging tempest who broke all crooked wings. He feared not His persecutors nor His enemies. He suffered not before His killers. Free and brave and daring He was. He defied all despots and oppressors. He saw the contagious pustules and amputated them. . . . He muted Evil

214

and He crushed Falsehood and He choked Treachery.

Jesus came not from the heart of the circle of Light to destroy the homes and build upon their ruins the convents and monasteries. He did not persuade the strong man to become a monk or a priest, but He came to send forth upon this earth a new spirit, with power to crumble the foundation of any monarchy built upon human bones and skulls. . . . He came to demolish the majestic palaces, constructed upon the graves of the weak, and crush the idols, erected upon the bodies of the poor. Jesus was not sent here to teach the people to build magnificent churches and temples amidst the cold wretched huts and dismal hovels. . . . He came to make the human heart a temple, and the soul an altar, and the mind a priest.

These were the missions of Jesus the Nazarene, and these are the teachings for which He was crucified. And if Humanity were wise, she would stand today and sing in strength the song of conquest and the hymn of triumph.

\*      \*      \*      \*      \*

Oh, Crucified Jesus, Who art looking sorrow-fully from Mount Calvary at the sad procession of the Ages, and hearing the clamour of the dark nations, and understanding the dreams of Eternity . . . Thou art, on the Cross, more glorious and dignified than one thousand kings upon one thousand thrones in one thousand empires. . . . .

Thou art, in the agony of death, more powerful than one thousand generals in one thousand wars. . . .

With Thy sorrows, Thou art more joyous than Spring with its flowers. . . .

With Thy suffering, Thou art more bravely silent than the crying angels of heaven. . . .

Before Thy lashers, Thou art more resolute than the mountain of rock. . . .

Thy wreath of thorns is more brilliant and sublime than the crown of Bahram. . . . The nails piercing Thy hands are more beautiful than the sceptre of Jupiter. . . .

The spatters of blood upon Thy feet are more resplendent than the necklace of Ishtar.

Forgive the weak who lament Thee today, for

216

they do not know how to lament themselves. . . .

Forgive them, for they do not know that Thou
hast conquered death with death, and bestowed
life upon the dead. . . .

Forgive them, for they do not know that Thy
strength still awaits them. . . .

Forgive them, for they do not know that every
day is Thy day.

Eventide of the Feast

# Eventide of the Feast

NIGHT HAD FALLEN and obscurity engulfed the city while the lights glittered in the palaces and the huts and the shops. The multitudes, wearing their festive raiment, crowded the streets and upon their faces appeared the signs of celebration and contentment.

I avoided the clamour of the throngs and walked alone, contemplating the Man Whose greatness they were honouring, and meditating the Genius of the Ages Who was born in poverty, and lived virtuously, and died on the Cross.

I was pondering the burning torch which was lighted in this humble village in Syria by the Holy Spirit. . . . The Holy Spirit Who hovers over all the ages, and penetrates one civilization and then another through His truth.

As I reached the public garden, I seated myself on a rustic bench and commenced looking between the naked trees toward the crowded streets; I listened to the hymns and songs of the celebrants.

After an hour of deep thinking, I looked sidewise and was surprised to find a man sitting by me, holding a short branch with which he engraved vague figures on the ground. I was startled, for I had not seen nor heard his approach, but I said within myself, "He is solitary, as I am." And after looking thoroughly at him, I saw that in spite of his old-fashioned raiment and long hair, he was a dignified man, worthy of attention. It seemed that he detected the thoughts within me, for in a deep and quiet voice he said, "Good evening, my son."

"Good evening to you," I responded with respect.

And he resumed his drawing while the strangely soothing sound of his voice was still echoing in my ears. And I spoke to him again, saying, "Are you a stranger in this city?"

"Yes, I am a stranger in this city and every city," he replied. I consoled him, adding, "A stranger should forget that he is an outsider in these holi-

222

days, for there is kindness and generosity in the people." He replied wearily, "I am more a stranger in these days than in any other." Having thus spoken, he looked at the clear skies; his eyes probed the stars and his lips quivered as if he had found in the firmament an image of a distant country. His queer statement aroused my interest, and I said, "This is the time of the year when the people are kind to all other people. The rich remember the poor and the strong have compassion for the weak."

He returned, "Yes, the momentary mercy of the rich upon the poor is bitter, and the sympathy of the strong toward the weak is naught but a reminder of superiority."

I affirmed, "Your words have merit, but the weak poor do not care to know what transpires in the heart of the rich, and the hungry never think of the method by which the bread he is craving is kneaded and baked."

And he responded, "The one who receives is not mindful, but the one who gives bears the burden of cautioning himself that it is with a view to brotherly love, and toward friendly aid, and not to self-esteem."

I was amazed at his wisdom, and again commenced to meditate upon his ancient appearance and strange garments. Then I returned mentally and said, "It appears that you are in need of help; will you accept a few coins from me?" And with a sad smile he answered me, saying, "Yes, I am in desperate need, but not of gold or silver."

Puzzled, I asked, "What is it that you require?"

"I am in need of shelter. I am in need of a place where I ran rest my head and my thoughts."

"Please accept these two denars and go to the inn for lodging," I insisted.

Sorrowfully he answered, "I have tried every inn, and knocked at every door, but in vain. I have entered every food shop, but none cared to help me. I am hurt, not hungry; I am disappointed, not tired; I seek not a roof, but human shelter."

I said within myself, "What a strange person he is! Once he talks like a philosopher and again like a madman!" As I whispered these thoughts into the ears of my inner self, he stared at me, lowered his voice to a sad level, and said, "Yes, I am a madman, but even a madman will find himself a stranger without shelter and hungry without food, for the heart of man is empty."

I apologized to him, saying, "I regret my unwitting thought. Would you accept my hospitality and take shelter in my quarters?"

"I knocked at your door and all the doors one thousand times, and received no answer," he answered severely.

Now I was convinced that he was truly a madman, and I suggested, "Let us go now, and proceed to my home."

He lifted his head slowly and said, "If you were aware of my identity you would not invite me to your home."

"Who are you?" I inquired, fearfully, slowly.

With a voice that sounded like the roar of the ocean, he thundered, bitterly, "I am the revolution who builds what the nations destroy. . . . I am the tempest who uproots the plants, grown by the ages. . . . I am the one who came to spread war on earth and not peace, for man is content only in misery!"

And, with tears coursing down his cheeks, he stood up high, and a mist of light grew about him, and he stretched forth his arms, and I saw the marks of the nails in the palms of his hands; I prostrated myself before him convulsively and cried out, saying, "Oh Jesus, the Nazarene!"

And He continued, in anguish, "The people are celebrating in My honour, pursuing the tradition woven by the ages around My name, but as to Myself, I am a stranger wandering from East to West upon this earth, and no one knows of Me. The foxes have their holes, and the birds of the skies their nests, but the Son of Man has no place to rest His head."

At that moment, I opened my eyes, lifted my head, and looked around, but found naught except a column of smoke before me, and I heard only the shivering voice of the silence of the night, coming from the depths of Eternity. I collected myself and looked again to the singing throngs in the distance, and a voice within me said, "The very strength that protects the heart from injury is the strength that prevents the heart from enlarging to its intended greatness within. The song of the voice is sweet, but the song of the heart is the pure voice of heaven."

# The Grave Digger

# The Grave Digger

In the terrible silence of the night, as all heavenly things disappeared behind the grasping veil of thick clouds, I walked lonely and afraid in the Valley of the Phantoms of Death.

As midnight came, and the spectres leaped about me with their horrible, ribbed wings, I observed a giant ghost standing before me, fascinating me with his hypnotic ghastliness. In a thundering voice he said, "Your fear is two-fold! You fear being in fear of me! You cannot conceal it, for you are weaker than the thin thread of the spider. What is your earthly name?"

I leaned against a great rock, gathered myself from this sudden shock, and in a sickly, trembling voice replied, "My name is Abdallah, which means 'slave of God.'" For a few moments he remained silent with a frightening silence. I grew accustomed to his appearance, but was again

231

shaken by his weird thoughts and words, his strange beliefs and contemplations.

He rumbled, "Numerous are the slaves of God, and great are God's woes with His slaves. Why did not your father call you 'Master of Demons' instead, adding one more disaster to the huge calamity of earth? You cling with terror to the small circle of gifts from your ancestors, and your affliction is caused by your parents' bequest, and you will remain a slave of death until you become one of the dead.

"Your vocations are wasteful and deserted, and your lives are hollow. Real life has never visited you, nor will it; neither will your deceitful self realize your living death. Your illusioned eyes see the people quivering before the tempest of life and you believe them to be alive, while in truth they have been dead since they were born. There were none who would bury them, and the one good career for you is that of grave digger, and as such you may rid the few living of the corpses heaped about the homes, the paths, and the churches."

I protested, "I cannot pursue such a vocation.

My wife and children require my support and companionship."

He leaned toward me, showing his braided muscles that seemed as the roots of a strong oak tree, abounding with life and energy, and he bellowed, "Give to each a spade and teach them to dig graves; your life is naught but black misery hidden behind walls of white plaster. Join us, for we genii are the only possessors of reality! The digging of graves brings a slow but positive benefit which causes the vanishing of the dead creatures who tremble with the storm and never walk with it." He mused and then inquired, "What is your religion?"

Bravely I stated, "I believe in God and I honour His prophets; I love virtue and I have faith in eternity."

With remarkable wisdom and conviction he responded, "These empty words were placed on human lips by past ages and not by knowledge, and you actually believe in yourself only; and you honour none but yourself, and you have faith only in the eternity of your desires. Man has worshipped

233

his own self since the beginning, calling that self by appropriate titles, until now, when he employs the word 'God' to mean that same self." Then the giant roared with laughter, the echoes reverberating through the hollows of the caverns, and he taunted, "How strange are those who worship their own selves, their real existence being naught but earthly carcasses!"

He paused, and I contemplated his sayings and meditated their meanings. He possessed a knowledge stranger than life and more terrible than death, and deeper than truth. Timidly, I ventured, "Do you have a religion or a God?"

"My name is The Mad God," he offered, "and I was born at all times, and I am the god of my own self. I am not wise, for wisdom is a quality of the weak. I am strong, and the earth moves under the steps of my feet, and when I stop, the procession of stars stops with me. I mock at the people. . . . I accompany the giants of night. . . . I mingle with the great kings of the genii. . . . I am in possession of the secrets of existence and non-existence.

234

"In the morning I blaspheme the sun . . . at noontide I curse humanity . . . at eventide I submerge nature . . . at night I kneel and worship myself. I never sleep, for I am time, the sea, and myself. . . . I eat human bodies for food, drink their blood to quench my thirst, and use their dying gasps to draw my breath. Although you deceive yourself, you are my brother and you live as I do. Begone . . . hypocrite! Crawl back to earth and continue to worship your own self amid the living dead!"

I staggered from the rocky, cavernous valley in narcotic bewilderment, scarcely believing what my ears had heard and my eyes had seen! I was torn in pain by some of the truths he had spoken, and wandered through the fields all that night in melancholy contemplation.

*     *     *     *     *

I procured a spade and said within myself, "Dig deeply the graves. . . . Go, now, and wherever you find one of the living dead, bury him in the earth."

Since that day I have been digging graves and burying the living dead. But the living dead are numerous and I am alone, having none to aid me. . . .

# Honeyed Poison

# Honeyed Poison

IT WAS a beautiful morn of dizzying brilliance in North Lebanon when the people of the village of Tula gathered around the portico of the small church that stood in the midst of their dwellings. They were discussing busily the sudden and unexplained departure of Farris Rahal, who left behind his bride of but half a year.

Farris Rahal was the Sheik and leader of the village, and he had inherited this honourable status from his ancestors who had ruled over Tula for centuries. Although he was not quite twenty-seven years of age, he possessed an outstanding ability and sincerity that won the admiration, reverence, and respect of all the fellahin. When Farris married Susan, the people commented upon him, saying, "What a fortunate man is Farris Rahal! He has attained all that man can hope for in the bounty of life's happiness, and he is but a youth!"

That morning, when all of Tula arose from slumber and learned that the Sheik had gathered his gold, mounted his steed and left the village bidding none farewell, curiosity and concern prevailed, and inquiries were many as to the cause that prompted him to desert his wife and his home, his lands and his vineyards.

\*　　\*　　\*　　\*　　\*

By reason of tradition and geography, life in North Lebanon is highly sociable, and the people share their joys and sorrows, provoked by humble spirit and instinctive clannishness. Upon any occurrence, the entire populace of the village convenes to inquire upon the incident, offers all possible assistance, and returns to labour until fate again offers a congregant mission.

It was such a matter that drew the people of Tula from their work that day, and caused them to gather about the church of Mar Tula discussing

240

the departure of their Sheik and exchanging views upon its singularity.

It was at this time that Father Estephan, head of the local church, arrived, and upon his drawn countenance one could read the unmistakable signs of deep suffering, the signs of a painfully wounded spirit. He contemplated the scene for a moment and then spoke. "Do not ask . . . do not ask any question of me! Before daybreak this day, Sheik Farris knocked upon the door of my house, and I saw him holding the rein of his horse, and from his face emanated grave sorrow and agonized grief. Upon my remark as to the strangeness of the hour, he replied, 'Father, I come to bid you farewell, for I am sailing beyond the oceans and will never again return to this land.' And he handed to me a sealed envelope, addressed to his dearest friend Nabih Malik, asking me to deliver it. He mounted his steed and sped off to the east, affording me no further opportunity to understand the purpose of his unusual departure."

One of the villagers observed, "Undoubtedly the missive will reveal to us the secret of his going, for Nabih is his closest friend." Another added, "Have you seen his bride, Father?" The priest replied, saying, "I visited her after the morning prayer and found her standing at the window, staring with unseeing eyes at something invisible, appearing as one who has lost all senses, and when I endeavoured to ask concerning Farris she merely said, 'I do not know! I do not know!' Then she wept like a child who suddenly becomes an orphan."

As the father concluded talking, the group tightened with fear at the startling report of a gunshot coming from the east portion of the village, and it was followed immediately by the bitter wailing of a woman. The throng was in a dismayed trance of immobility for a moment, and then, men, women and children, all ran toward the scene, and upon their faces there was a dark mask of fear and evil omen. As they reached the garden that surrounded the Sheik's residence, they became witness to a most horrible drama, portrayed with death. Nabih Malik was lying on the ground, a stream of blood issuing from his breast, and by him stood Susan, wife of the Sheik Farris Rahal, tearing her hair and shredding her raiment and flailing her arms about and shrieking wildly, "Nabih . . . Nabih . . . why did you do it!"

The onlookers were astounded, and it was as though the unseen hands of fate had clutched with icy fingers at their hearts. The priest found in the dead Nabih's right hand the note he had delivered that morning, and he placed it deftly into his robe without notice by the milling multitude.

Nabih was carried to his miserable mother, who, upon seeing the lifeless body of her only son, lost her sanity in shock and soon joined him in Eternity. Susan was led slowly into her home, wavering between faltering life and grasping death.

As Father Estephan reached his home, under bent shoulders, he fastened the door, adjusted his reading glasses, and in a quivering whisper commenced reading to himself the message he had taken from the hand of the departed Nabih.

"My Dearest Friend Nabih,

"I must leave this village of my fathers, for my continued presence is casting misery upon you and upon my wife and upon myself. You are noble in spirit, and scorn the betrayal of friend or neighbour, and although I know that Susan is innocent and virtuous, I know also that the true love which unites your heart and her heart is beyond your power and beyond my hopes. I cannot struggle longer against the mighty will of God, as I cannot halt the strong flow of the great Kadeesha River.

"You have been my sincere friend, Nabih, since we played as children in the fields; and before God, believe me, you remain my friend. I beg you to ponder with good thoughts upon me in the future as you did in the past. Tell Susan that I love her and that I wronged her by taking her in empty marriage. Tell her that my heart bled in burning pain each time I turned from restless sleep in the silence of the night and observed her kneeling before the shrine of Jesus, weeping and beating upon her bosom in anguish.

"There is no punishment so severe as that suf-

244

fered by the woman who finds herself imprisoned between a man she loves and another man who loves her. Susan suffered through a constant and painful conflict, but performed sorrowfully and honourably and silently her duties as a wife. She tried, but could not choke her honest love for you.

"I am leaving for distant lands and will never again return, for I can no longer act as barrier to a genuine and eternal love, embraced by the enfolded arms of God; and may God, in his inscrutable wisdom, protect and bless both of you.

"FARRIS"

Father Estephan folded the letter, returned it to his pocket, and sat by the window that opened upon the distant valley. He sailed long and deep in a great ocean of contemplation, and after wise and intense meditation, he stood suddenly, as if he had found between the plaited folds of his intricate thoughts a delicate and horrible secret, disguised with diabolical slyness, and wrapped with elaborate cunning! He cried out, "How sagacious you are, Farris! How massive, yet simple,

245

is your crime! You sent to him honey blended with fatal poison, and enclosed death in a letter! And when Nabih pointed the weapon at his heart, it was your finger that discharged the missile, and it was your will that engulfed his will. . . . How clever you are, Farris!"

He returned quivering to his chair, shaking his head and combing his beard with his fingers, and upon his lips appeared a smile whose meaning was more terrible than the tragedy itself. He opened his prayer book and commenced reading and pondering, and at intervals he raised his head to hear the wailing and lamentations of the women, coming from the heart of the village of Tula, close by the Holy Cedars of Lebanon.

Iram, the City of Lofty Pillars

# Iram, the City of Lofty Pillars

TRANSLATOR'S PROLOGUE

*"Seest thou not how thy God*
*Dealt with Ad of Iram, with*
*Lofty pillars, the like of*
*Which were not produced in*
*All of existence?"*
            The Holy Quran.

THE AD PEOPLE, with their Prophet Hud, are cited often in the Holy Quran, and their traditions belong to ancient Arabia. Their eponymous ancestor Ad was fourth in generation from Noah, having been a son of Aus, who was the son of Aram, who was the son of Shem, who was the first son of Noah.

They occupied a great tract of southern Arabia,

extending from *Umman* at the mouth of the Persian Gulf to *Hadramaut* and *Yemen* at the southern end of the Red Sea, and the long, twisting areas of *ahqaf* (sands) in their domain were irrigated by canals.

The people were of great physical stature, and were excellent masons and builders. However, as so often happens, their vast advancements resulted in the forsaking of the true God, and the leaders anguished the people with oppression in its most severe state.

A three year famine visited them, but they took no warning, and at length a terrible and tremendous blast of searing wind destroyed them and their civilization. A remnant, known as the Second Ad, or *Thamud,* salvaged itself and survived, but later suffered a similar fate, presumably because of the sins of the people.

The tomb of the Prophet Hud (*Qabr Nabi Hud*) is still shown to visitors in *Hadramaut,* latitude 16 degrees north, longitude 49½ degrees east, about 90 miles north of *Mukalla.* Ruins and inscriptions abound in the general vicinity, and there is an annual pilgrimage to this site in the month of *Rajab*.*

Iram appears to have been an ancient Ad capital in southern Arabia, and it boasted lofty architecture. Controversially, some archaeologists and historians believe Iram to be the name of an individual hero of the Ad, and if this be true, the descriptive phrase "lofty pillars" applies not to the edifices, but to the people themselves, for the Ad were a tall race.

This sector, sometimes called *Arabia Felix,* is a source of interest, devotion and prosperity to many Arabs, for in its many ancient remains, numerous objects of historical, religious, and monetary value have been found. In the time of *Muawiya* a rich cache of precious stones was discovered, and more recently some gold, silver, and bronze pieces of statuary bearing Sabaean inscriptions came to light in *Najram*. These have been described in detail in the British Museum Quarterly, Volume 4, September 1937.

---

* Bibliography: "Hadramaut—its Mysteries Unveiled," by D. Van Der Meulen and H. Von Wissman, Leyden, 1932. (Editor's note.)

The source of the foregoing lineage and geography is the Holy Quran. Kahlil Gibran probably based his play "Iram, the City of Lofty Pillars" on this information, or upon similar Eastern mythology pursuing the general vein of the following brief Arabian fantasy:

"When Shaddad, the son of Ad, became the Great King of the World, he commanded one thousand Emirs to seek for him a vast land abundant with water and pure air, that he might build in it a Golden City afar from the mountains. The rulers roamed throughout the world in quest of such land, and each Emir took with him one thousand men.

"And when it was found, the architects and builders erected within it a square city of forty leagues. They built a huge wall extending five hundred cubits, made of onyx stones, and covered it with sheets of gold that misted the eyes when the sun shone.

"And King Shaddad despatched his people to all parts of the world, and commanded them to dig out gold from the ground, to be used as mortar for the bricks. And he built inside the city walls one hundred thousand palaces for one hundred thousand officials of his kingdom. Each palace was erected upon columns of chrysolite and ruby blended with gold, and each column reached one hundred cubits toward heaven.

"And the rivers were brought through the city, and their tributaries through the palaces. The roadways of the city were gold and precious stones and ruby, and the palaces were adorned richly with gold and silver. Trees were imbedded along the banks of the river, and their branches were of living gold, and their leaves of silver, and their fruits of onyx and pearls. And the walls of the palaces were embellished with musk and ambergris.

"And King Shaddad built for himself a garden whose trees were of emerald and ruby, and upon the branches were singing birds of pure gold."

*     *     *     *     *

# THE PLAY

IRAM, THE CITY OF LOFTY PILLARS

*The locale of the play:* A small forest of walnut, pomegranate and poplar trees. In this forest, between the Orantes River (Nahr el'Asi) and the village of Hermil, stands an old solitary house in a clearing.

*The time of the play:* Late afternoon in mid-July, 1883.

*The characters of the play:*

    Zain Abedeen of Nahawand, forty years old, who is a Persian Dervish and a mystic.

    Najeeb Rahmé, thirty years old, a Lebanese scholar.

    Amena Divine, age unknown, prophetic and mysterious, known in the vicinity as the Houri of the Valley.

    \*     \*     \*     \*     \*

As the curtain rises, Zain Abedeen is seen leaning his head on one hand, under the trees, and with his long walking staff is inscribing circular

254

figures upon the ground. Najeeb Rahmé enters
the clearing on a horse a few moments thereafter.
He dismounts, fastens the rein to the trunk of a
tree, dusts his clothes and approaches Zain Abedeen.

Najeeb: Peace be with you, Sir!
Zain: And with you be peace. (*He turns his face
aside and whispers to himself*): Peace we
shall accept . . . but superiority? That is a
different matter.
Najeeb: Is this the abiding place of Amena Divine?
Zain: This is but one of her several abodes. She
lives in none, yet she exists in all.
Najeeb: I have inquired of many, yet none knew
Amena Divine had numerous dwellings.
Zain: This establishes that your informants are
people who cannot see except with their eyes,
nor hear except through their ears. Amena
Divine is everywhere (*points to the east with
his staff*) and she roams the knolls and the
valleys.

255

Najeeb: Will she return to this place today?

Zain: Heaven so willing, she will return here today.

Najeeb: (*Seating himself upon a rock before Zain, and staring at him*): Your beard reveals to me that you are a Persian.

Zain: Yes, I was born in Nahawand, reared in Sheezar, and educated in Nisabour. I journeyed through the east and west of the world and returned, for I found myself a stranger to all places.

Najeeb: We are often strangers to ourselves!

Zain: (*Disregarding Najeeb's comment*): Truly, I have encountered and conversed with thousands of men, and could find none but those who are content with their close environs, confining themselves to their small prisons which are the only ones they know and see in this vast world.

Najeeb: (*Bewildered by Zain's words*): Is not man naturally attached to the place of his birth?

Zain: The person who is limited in heart and

256

thought is inclined to love that which is limited in life, and the weak-sighted cannot see more than one cubit ahead upon the path he treads, nor more than one cubit of the wall upon which he rests his shoulder.

Najeeb: Not all of us are enabled to see with our inner eyes the greath depths of life, and it is cruel to demand that the weak-sighted see the dim and the far.

Zain: You are correct, but is it not also cruel to press wine from the green grape?

Najeeb: (*After a brief, contemplative silence*): For many years I have been hearing tales of Amena Divine. I was fascinated with these stories, and determined to meet her and inquire into her secrets and mysteries.

Zain: There is no person in this world who is capable of possessing the secrets of Amena Divine, just as there is no human capable of roaming the bottom of the sea as if walking in a garden.

Najeeb: I beg your pardon, Sir, for I have not rendered clear my purpose. I know that I am not capable of acquiring for myself the unrevealed mysteries of Amena Divine. My prime hope is that she will relate to me the story of her entry into Iram, the City of Lofty Pillars, and the manner of things she found in this Golden City.

Zain: You need merely to stand in sincerity at the door of her dream. If it opens, you will reach your goal, and if it does not open, then your own self must bear blame.

Najeeb: I fail to comprehend your strange words.

Zain: They are simple . . . simple by comparison to your great reward should you succeed. Amena Divine knows more about the people than they know about themselves, and she can perceive in one glance all of that which is hidden within them. If she finds you worthy, she will be happy to converse with you and place you upon the true pathway to light. If not, she will ignore you with a strength bespeaking your non-existence.

Najeeb: What shall I do and what shall I say in order to prove myself worthy?

Zain: It is vain and wasteful to endeavour an approach to Amena Divine through mere words or deeds, for she neither listens nor sees. But through the soul of her ear she will hear what you do not say, and through the soul of her eye she will see what you do not do.

Najeeb: How wise and how beautiful are your words!

Zain: Were I to talk of Amena Divine for a century, all I would say would be naught but the humming of a mute who struggles to sing a song of beauty.

Najeeb: Do you know where this strange woman was born?

Zain: Her body was born in the vicinity of Damascus, but all else, greater than substance, was born in the bosom of God.

Najeeb: What of her parents?

Zain: Can that be of consequence? Can you study the element properly by examining its surface alone? Can you foretell the taste of the wine by gazing upon the vessel?

259

Najeeb: You speak the truth. Nevertheless, there must be a bond between the spirit and the body, as there is a bond between the body and its immediate surroundings; and while I place no faith in chance, I believe that a knowledge of the background of Amena Divine will be of value to me in probing the secret of her life.

Zain: Well spoken! I know naught concerning her mother, except that she died upon the birth of Amena, her only child. Her father was Sheik Abdul Ghany, the famous blind prophet, who was thought to be divine, and recognized as the Imam of his time in mysticism. May his soul receive God's mercy! He was fanatically attached to his daughter, and educated her carefully and poured into her heart all of his heart. And as she grew, he sought that she take from him all of his knowledge and wisdom. In truth, his great learning was slight compared to that knowledge which God had already bestowed upon Amena. And of his daughter he said, "From my painful darkness there came a great light that illuminated my pathway through life." When Amena was twenty-three years old, her father took her with him on a pilgrimage, and when they crossed the Damascus Desert and made their way into the wasteland, and the lighted city disappeared behind them, the blind father became fevered and died. Amena buried him and watched over his grave for seven days and seven nights, calling to his spirit and inquiring into hidden secrets of his soul. And on the seventh night the spirit of her father dismissed her from her vigil and commanded her to travel to the southeast, whereupon she obeyed. (*Zain ceases talking, gazes at the distant horizon, and after a few moments continues*): She resumed the journey and fought her way until she reached the heart of the desert, which they call Rabh el Khali, and which no caravan in my knowledge has ever crossed. A few wanderers are said to have reached this place in the early days of the Islamic religion.

The pilgrims believed Amena to have been lost, and mourned her as having died in hunger, and upon their return, told the populace of Damascus of the tragedy. All those who had known Sheik Abdul Ghany and his strange daughter lamented them, but as the years passed, they were forgotten. Five years thereafter, Amena Divine appeared in Musil, and because of her supernatural wisdom, knowledge, and beauty, her presence enraptured the people like a silver chip of heaven's night falling from the blue tent.

Najeeb: (*Interrupting, although obviously interested in Zain's story*): Did Amena reveal her identity to the people?

Zain: She disclosed nothing concerning herself. She stood with unveiled face before the Imams and scholars, speaking of divine and immortal things, and describing to them the City of Lofty Pillars in a manner so eloquent as to surprise and captivate her listeners, and the number of her followers increased with each day.

The wise men of the city became envious and complained to the Emir, who summoned her to appear before him, and upon her appearance, he placed in her hands a packet of gold and urged her to depart the borders of the city. She refused to accept the gold and, alone, left the city under the cover of night. She journeyed through Constantinople, Damascus, Homs, and Tripoli, and in every city she brought light into the hearts of the people who gathered about her, drawn by her magic power. However, the Imams of each city opposed her, and continual exile was her lot.

Finally, upon deciding to lead a solitary life, she came to this place a few years ago. She denied herself all things except the love of God and her meditations upon His mysteries. This is but a small picture of the history of Amena Divine. But the blessed power given me by God to understand something of her ideal existence is the same power which, in its overwhelming intoxication of heart, renders me unable to describe in earthly words the wonders of Amena Divine. What human is able to gather in one cup the total wisdom that surrounds this world in many cups?

Najeeb: My gratitude, Sir, for the interesting and vital information you have offered. My anxiety to see her is now greater than ever!

Zain: (*Staring at Najeeb with piercing eyes*): You are a Christian, are you not?

Najeeb: Yes, I was born a Christian. However, with all regard to my ancestors, who bequeathed to me a religion as well as a name, I must add that if we were to do away with the various religions, we would find ourselves united and enjoying one great faith and religion, abounding in brotherhood.

Zain: You speak wisely, and on the matter of a united faith, there is none more abundantly informed than Amena Divine. She is, to the multitudes of all beliefs and ancestries, like the dew of the morn that falls from high and becomes as glittering gems upon the colourful leaves of all of the flowers. Yes . . .

she is like the morning dew. . . . (*Zain stops talking at this point, and looks toward the east, listening carefully. Then he stands up, cautioning Najeeb to be alert, and Zain warns in an excited whisper*): Amena Divine approaches! May good fortune be with you!

Najeeb: (*In a faltering whisper*): My long months of anxiety may soon find reward! (*Najeeb places his hand upon his forehead, as if to calm his leaping nerves, and he senses a change in the character of the atmosphere. Recalling Zain's words of possible failure, his expression of joyful anticipation changes to one of deep concern, but he now remains as motionless as a statue of marble.*)

(*Amena Divine enters and stands before the two men. She is draped in long, silken robes, and her features, gestures, and raiment cause her to resemble one of those goddesses worshipped by the past ages, rather than an oriental woman of her actual time. It is impossible to speculate even generally upon her age, for her face, though youthful, is unrevealing, and her deep eyes reflect one thousand years of wisdom and suffering. Najeeb and Zain remain reverently motionless, as if in the presence of one of the prophets of God.*)

Amena: (*After staring at Najeeb as if penetrating his heart with her magnificent eyes; in a serene, confident voice*): You are here to learn about us, but you shall not know more about us than you know about yourself, and you shall hear from us only that which you hear from yourself.

Najeeb: (*Perplexed, and exhibiting nervous fear*): I have already seen, heard, and believed. . . . I am contented.

Amena: Be not satisfied with partial contentment, for he who engulfs the spring of life with one empty jar will depart with two full jars. (*Amena extends her hand toward him; he takes it in awe with both hands and kisses the ends of her fingers, impelled by a strong, unknown emotion. She then offers her other hand to Zain Abedeen, and he kisses it. Na-*

*jeeb appears happy to have pursued the apparently correct procedure first. Amena Divine slowly withdraws herself.*)

Amena: (*Sits upon a smooth rock and speaks to Najeeb*): These are the chairs of God. Be seated. (*Najeeb seats himself nearby and Zain does likewise. Amena continues, again to Najeeb*): We see in your eyes the true light of God, and he who looks upon the true light of God will see in us our inner reality. You are sincere, and you love the truth, and therefore you desire to know more of truth. If you have words to say, you have but to speak and we will give heed, and if you have in your heart a question, ask and we will respond in truth.

Najeeb: I come to inquire upon a matter that has been the consuming topic of conversation among the throngs. But when I found myself in your presence, I realized the enormity of the meaning of life, truth, and God, and now all else is unimportant. I am like the fisherman who threw his net into the sea hoping

267

to find it laden with food for a day of his sustenance, but when he drew the net he found in it a heap of everlasting precious stones.

Amena: I see in your heart that you have heard about our entry into Iram, the City of Lofty Pillars, and that you desire now to hear further of the Golden City.

Najeeb: (*Ashamed, yet intensely interested*): Yes, since childhood the name Iram, the City of Lofty Pillars has been embracing my dreams, preying upon my thoughts, and agitating my heart through its hidden meaning and tremendous significance.

Amena: (*Lifts her head and closes her eyes, and in a voice that, to Najeeb, seems to be emanating from the very heart of space, she speaks solemnly*): Yes, we reached and entered the Golden City and sojourned there and filled our souls with its fragrance, and our hearts with its secrets, and our pouches with its pearls and its rubies, and our ears with its music, and our eyes with its beauty.

And he who doubts that which we have seen and heard and found there is doubting his very self before God and man.

Najeeb: (*Slowly, and with difficulty and humility*): I am naught but an infant, lisping and faltering and unable to express myself. Will you be kind to me and explain further, and forgive my many questions?

Amena: Ask as you wish, for God has made many doors opening into truth which He opens to all who knock upon them with hands of faith.

Najeeb: Did you enter Iram, the City of Lofty Pillars in body or in spirit? Is this Golden City built of the glittering elements of this world and erected in a precise part of this world, or is it an imaginary or spiritual city which only the prophets of God can reach in ecstasy when Providence brings upon their souls a veil of eternity?

Amena: All on earth, seen and unseen, is spiritual only. I entered the Golden City with my body, which is merely an earthly manifestation of my greater spirit, and which is, in all persons, a temporary vault for the safe-keeping of the spirit. I entered Iram with my body concealed within my spirit, for both are ever-present while on earth, and he who endeavours to cleave the body from the spirit, or the spirit from the body is directing his heart away from truth. The flower and its fragrance are one, and the blind who deny the colour and the image of the flower, believing that it possesses only a fragrance vibrating the ether, are like those with pinched nostrils who believe that flowers are naught but pictures and colours, possessing no fragrance.

Najeeb: Then Iram, the City of Lofty Pillars, is a spiritual place only!

Amena: (*Indulgently*): Time and place are spiritual states, and all that is seen and heard is spiritual. If you close your eyes you will perceive all things through the depths of your inner self, and you will see the world, physical and ethereal, in its intended entirety, and you will acquaint yourself with its necessary laws and precautions, and you will understand the greatness that it possesses beyond its closeness. Yes . . . if you will close your eyes and open your heart and your inner perception you will discover the beginning and the end of existence . . . that beginning which in its turn becomes an ending, and that ending which must surely become a beginning.

Najeeb: Is every human capable of thus closing his eyes and seeing the unclothed truth of life and existence?

Amena: Man is empowered by God to hope and hope fervently, until that for which he is hoping takes the cloak of oblivion from his eyes, whereupon he will at last view his real self. And he who sees his real self sees the truth of real life for himself, for all humanity, and for all things.

Najeeb: (*Placing both hands upon his bosom*): Then all I can see and hear and touch and think of in this universe exists right here in my own heart!

Amena: All things in this vast universe exist in you, with you, and for you.

Najeeb: Then I may truthfully say that Iram, the City of Lofty Pillars is not far distant, but is found within *me,* the entity existing as Najeeb Rahmé!

Amena: All things in this creation exist within you, and all things in you exist in creation; there is no border between you and the closest things, and there is no distance between you and the farthest things, and all things, from the lowest to the loftiest, from the smallest to the greatest, are within you as equal things. In one atom are found all the elements of the earth; in one motion of the mind are found the motions of all the laws of existence; in one drop of water are found the secrets of all of the endless oceans; in one aspect of *you* are found all the aspects of *existence.*

Najeeb: (*Overwhelmed by the vastness of the subject, and after a brief pause, permitting full assimilation of his instruction*): I was told

272

that you journeyed many days before you reached the heart of the desert of Rabh el Khali, and that your father's spirit revealed itself to you and directed you in your wanderings until you reached the Golden City. If a person should desire to reach that city, need he be in the same spiritual state you possessed at that time, and is it required that he possess your wisdom in order to gain entrance into that celestial place you visited?

Amena: We crossed the desert and suffered the pangs of hunger and the madness of thirst and the fears of the day and the horrors of the night and the frightening silence of eternity before we saw the walls of the Golden City. But many are those who reached the city of God before us without walking one cubit, and they reveled in its beauty and brightness without sorrowing in body or spirit. Truly I say unto you that many have visited the Sacred City although they never left the places of their birth.

*(Amena Divine interrupts herself and re-*

273

*mains silent for a moment. Then she points at the trees and myrtles about her and continues*): For every seed that autumn drops into the heart of the earth, there exists a different manner of splitting the shell from the pulp; then are created the leaves, and then the flowers, and then the fruit. But regardless of the fashion in which this takes place, these plants must undertake one sole pilgrimage, and their great mission is to stand before the face of the sun.

Zain (*Moves gracefully back and forth, impressed by Amena as if in a supreme world. In an inspired voice he cries out prayerfully*): God is great! There is no God but Allah, the Merciful, who knows our needs!

Amena: Allah is great . . . there is no God but Allah . . . there is nothing but Allah!

Zain: (*Repeats Amena's words in a scarcely audible whisper, with fervent, visible trembling*).

Najeeb: (*Stares at Amena Divine as if in a trance, and in a strong, defiant voice says*): There is no God but *God*!

274

Amena: (*Surprised*): There is no God but *Allah* . . . there is nothing but *Allah*. You may speak these words and remain a Christian, for a God Who is good knows of no segregations amongst words or names, and were a God to deny His blessing to those who pursue a different path to eternity, then there is no human who should offer worship.*

Najeeb: (*Bends his head, closes his eyes and repeats Amena's words of prayer to Allah. He raises his head, saying*): I shall say the words to the God who offers me the true pathway to Him, and I shall continue to say them to Him until the end of my life, for I am in search of truth. And my prayers to God are to *The God*, wherever He may be and whatever He may be called. I love God . . . all of my life will I love God.

Amena: Your life has no end, and you shall live forevermore.

---

* The zealous Christian in the Near East is taught that it is a sin to repeat any prayer belonging to the Islamic religion. (Editor's note.)

Najeeb: *Who* am I, and *what* am I, to live unto eternity?

Amena: You are *you,* and as such, you are a creature of God, and you are therefore everything.

Najeeb: Amena Divine, I know that the particles of which my own *self* is composed will remain as long as I remain, but will that *thought* which I call *myself* remain? Will this dim, new awakeness, garmented with the light slumber of dawn remain? Will these hopes and desires, sorrows and joys remain? Will these shivering fancies of my disturbed sleep, brilliant in truth's light, remain?

Amena: (*Raises her eyes toward heaven, as if reaching for something in the great pocket of space. In a clear, strong voice she speaks*): Each thing that exists remains forever, and the very existence of existence is proof of its eternity. But without that realization, which is the knowledge of perfect being, man would never know whether there was existence or non-existence. If eternal existence is altered, then it must become more beautiful; and if it disappears, it must return with more sublime image; and if it sleeps, it must dream of a better awakening, for it is ever greater upon its rebirth.

I feel pity toward those who admit of the eternity of the elements of which the eye is made, but at the same time doubt the eternity of the various objects of sight which employ the eye as a medium.

I feel sympathy for the one who divides life into two parts, and at the same time places faith in one part and doubts the other.

I am saddened by the one who gazes upon the mountains and plains upon which the sun throws its rays, and who listens to the breeze singing the song of the thin branches, and who inhales the fragrance of the flowers and the jasmine, and then says within himself, "No . . . what I see and hear will pass away, and what I know and feel will vanish." This humble soul who sees and contemplates reverently the joys and sorrows about him, and then denies the perpetuity of their existence, must himself vanish like vapour in the air and disappear, for he is seeking darkness and placing his back to truth. Verily, he is a living soul denying *his* very existence, for he denies *other* of God's existing things.

Najeeb: (*Excited*): Amena Divine, I believe in my existence, and he who listens to your words and does not believe is more the solid rock than a human in being.

Amena: God has placed in each soul a true guide to the great light, but man struggles to find life outside himself, unaware that the life he is seeking is within him.

Najeeb: Is there any light outside the body by which we can illuminate the way into our inner depths? Do we possess any power that will stir our spirits and awaken in us the realization of our living oblivion, and point the way to eternal knowledge? (*He becomes silent for a few moments, apparently fearful of proceeding. Then he continues, as if overcoming his reluctance*): Did not your father's

278

soul reveal to you the secret of the earthly imprisonment of the soul?

Amena: It is vain for the wayfarer to knock upon the door of the empty house. Man is standing mutely between the non-existence within him and the reality of his surroundings. If we did not possess what we have within ourselves we could not have the things we call our environs. My father's spirit called to me when my soul called to his soul, and revealed to my outer knowledge what my inner knowledge had already known.

Therefore, in simplicity, were it not for the hunger and thirst within me, I would not have obtained food and water from my environs; and were it not for the longing and affection within me, I would not have found the subject of my longing and affection about me in the Golden City.

Najeeb: Is every person able to spin a thread from the sinews of his longing and affection and attach it between his soul and a departed soul? Is there any endowed people, empowered to talk to the spirits and understand their will and purpose?

Amena: Between the people of eternity and the people of the earth there is a constant communication, and all comply with the will of that unseen power. Oftentimes an individual will perform an act, believing that it is born of his own free will, accord, and command, but in fact he is being guided and impelled with precision to do it. Many great men attained their glory by surrendering themselves in complete submission to the will of the spirit, employing no reluctance or resistance to its demands, as a violin surrenders itself to the complete will of a fine musician.

Between the spiritual world and the world of substance there is a path upon which we walk in a swoon of slumber. It reaches us and we are unaware of its strength, and when we return to ourselves we find that we are carrying with our real hands the seeds to be planted carefully in the good earth of our daily lives, bringing forth good deeds and words of beauty. Were it not for that path between our lives and the departed lives, no prophet or poet or learned man would have appeared among the people. (*Amena lowers her voice to a compelling whisper, and continues*): Truly I say unto you, and the outcome of time will prove it, that there are ties between the upper world and the lower world as surely as there is a binding tie between a mother and her child. We are surrounded with an intuitive atmosphere that attracts our inner consciousness, and a knowledge that cautions our judgment, and a power that strengthens our own power. I say unto you that our doubt does not disprove or fortify our surrender to that which we doubt, and the fact of busying ourselves in self-gratification will not divert us from the accomplishment by the spirits of their purpose; and blinding ourselves to the reality of our spiritual being will not conceal our spiritual being from the eyes of the universe; and if we stop walking, we are still walking if they are walking . . . and if we remain motionless, we are still moving with their moving . . . and if we silence ourselves, we are still speaking with their voices.

Our sleep cannot drive the influence of their awakeness from us, nor can our awakeness divert their dreams from the stages of our fancies, for we and they are two worlds embraced by one world . . . we and they are two spirits wrapped within one spirit . . . we and they are two existences united by one Supreme and Eternal Consciousness which is above all and without beginning and without ending.

Najeeb: (*Radiant, he is now thinking and feeling along the lines of Amena Divine's revelations*): Will ever the day arrive when man will discover through scientific knowledge and experience and earthly manifestation that which the spirits have always known through God, and which our hearts have known through longing? Must we await death in order to establish the eternity of our ideal selves? Will ever the day come when we will feel with the fingers of our hands those great secrets which we now feel only with the fingers of our faith?

Amena: Yes, that day will come. But how ignorant are those who see, without question, the abstract existence with *some* of their senses, but insist upon doubting until that existence reveals itself to *all* their senses. Is not faith the sense of the heart as truly as sight is the sense of the eye? And how narrow is the one who hears the song of the blackbird and sees it hovering above the branches, but doubts that which he has seen and heard until he seizes the bird with his hands. Were not a *portion* of his senses sufficient? How strange is the one who dreams in truth of a beautiful reality, and then, when he endeavours to fashion it into form but cannot succeed, doubts the dream and blasphemes the reality and distrusts the beauty!

How blind is the one who fancies and plans a matter in all true form and angles, and when he cannot prove it completely with superficial measurement and word proofs, believes that his idea and imagination were empty objects! But if he contemplates with sincerity and meditates upon these happenings, he will understand with conviction that his idea is as much a reality as is the bird of the sky, but that it is not yet crystallized, and that the idea is a segment of knowledge that cannot be proved with figures and words, for it is too high and too spacious to be imprisoned at that moment; too deeply imbedded in the spiritual to submit yet to the real.

Najeeb: (*Believing, yet curious*): Is there true being in all imagination, and real knowledge in every idea and fancy?

Amena: Verily, it is impossible for the mirror of the soul to reflect in the imagination anything which does not stand before it. It is impossible for the calm lake to show in its depth the figure of any mountain or the picture of any tree or cloud that does not exist close by the lake. It is impossible for the light to throw upon the earth a shadow of an object that has no being. Nothing can be seen, heard, or otherwise sensed unless it has actual *being*. When you *know* a thing, you *believe* it, and the true believer sees with his *spiritual discernment* that which the surface investigator cannot see with the eyes of his head, and he understands through his *inner* thought that which the outside examiner cannot understand with his demanding, acquired process of thought.

The believer acquaints himself with the sacred realities through deep senses different from those used by others. A believer looks upon his senses as a great wall surrounding him, and when he walks upon the path he says, "This city has no exit, but it is perfect within." (*Amena stands, walks toward Najeeb and, after a pause, says*): The believer lives for all the days and the nights, and the unfaithful live but a few hours.

How small is the life of the person who

places his hands between his face and the world, seeing naught but the narrow lines of his hands!

How unjust to themselves are those who turn their backs to the sun, and see naught except the shadows of their physical selves upon the earth!

Najeeb: (*Standing, in preparation for departure*): Shall I tell the people that Iram, the City of Lofty Pillars is a spiritual city of dreams, and that Amena Divine reached it through longing and affection for it, and through the door of faith?

Amena: Tell them that Iram, the City of Lofty Pillars is a true city, existing with the same visible existence of the oceans and the mountains and the forests and the deserts, for all in eternity is real. Tell them that Amena Divine reached it after she crossed the great desert and suffered the agonies of thirst, the torture of hunger, and the sorrows and horrors of aloneness. Tell them that the Golden City was erected by the giants of the ages from the glittering elements of existence, and concealed it not from the people, but the people cornered themselves from it. And tell them that the one who loses his way before reaching Iram must cast blame upon the guide, and not upon the rough, hard road. Tell them that the one who does not light his lamp of truth will find the road dark and impassable. (*Amena looks to heaven with love in her eyes, and her face emanates sweetness and peace*).

Najeeb: (*Approaches Amena slowly, with head bent low, takes her hand and whispers*): It is eventide, and I must return to the dwellings of the people before darkness engulfs the road.

Amena: Under God's direction, you will find your way in light.

Najeeb: I shall walk in the light of the great torch you have placed in my trembling hand.

Amena: Walk in the light of Truth, which cannot be extinguished by the tempest. (*Amena looks long and intently at Najeeb, her counte-*

*nance bearing the love of a mother. Then she leaves to the east, and walks amid the trees until she disappears from view).*

Zain: May I accompany you to the vicinity of the people?

Najeeb: With pleasure to me. I believed, however, that you lived close by Amena Divine. I envied you, saying within myself, "Would that I were to abide here."

Zain: We can live afar from the sun, but we cannot live close to the sun; yet, we need the sun. I come here often to be blessed and advised, and then I depart contented. *(Najeeb unties the rein and, leading his horse, walks off with Zain Abedeen.)*

*(Curtain)*

# The Day of My Birth

# The Day of My Birth

It was on this day of the year that my
Mother brought me into the world; on
This day, a quarter-century past, the
Great silence placed me between the arms
Of Existence, replete with lamentation
And tears and conflicts.

Twenty five times have I encircled the
Blazing sun, and many times more has the
Moon encircled my smallness; yet, I have
Not learned the secrets of light, neither
Do I comprehend the mystery of darkness.

I have journeyed these twenty five years
With the earth and the sun and the planets
Through the Supreme Infinite; yet, my soul
Yearns for understanding of the Eternal Law

As the hollow grotto reverberates with the
Echo of the waves of the sea, but never fills.

Life exists through the existence of the
Heavenly system, but is not aware of the
Unbounded might of the firmament; and the
Soul sings the praise of the ebb and flow
Of a heavenly melody, but does not perceive
Its meaning.

Twenty five years past, the hand of Time
Recorded my being, and I am a living page
In the book of the universe; yet, I am now
But naught; but a vague word with meaning
Of complication symbolizing now nothing,
And then many things.

Meditations and memories, on this day of
Each year, congest my soul and halt the
Procession of life, revealing to me the
Phantoms of wasted nights, and sweeping
Them away as the great wind disperses the
Thin cloud from the horizon. And they

Vanish in the obscured corner of my hut
As the murmur of the narrow stream must
Vanish in the distant, broadened valley.

On this day of each year, the spirits
Which have fashioned my soul visit with
Me from all of Eternity and gather about
Me, chanting the sorrowful hymns of memories.
Then they retreat swiftly and disappear
Behind the visible objects like a flock of
Birds descending upon a deserted threshing
Floor whereupon they find no seeds; they
Hover in disappointment and depart quickly
For a more rewarding place.

On this day I meditate upon the past,
Whose purpose puzzles me in mind and
Confuses me in heart, and I look
Upon it as I look into a hazy mirror
In which I see naught but death-like
Countenances upon the past years.
As I gaze again, I see my own self
Staring upon my sorrowful self, and

I question Sorrow but find him mute.
Sorrow, if able to speak, would
Prove sweeter than the joy of song.

During my twenty five years of life
I have loved many things, and often
I loved that which the people hated,
And loathed that which the people
Loved.

And that which I loved when I was a
Child, I still love, and shall continue
To love forevermore. The power to
Love is God's greatest gift to man,
For it never will be taken from the
Blessed one who loves.

I love death, and entitle it with
Sweet names, and praise it with
Loving words, secretly and to the
Throngs of taunting listeners.

Although I have not renounced my great
Allegiance to death, I became deeply

294

Enamoured with life also, for life and
Death are equal to me in charm and
Sweetness and attraction, and they
Have joined hands in fostering in me
My longings and affections, and in
Sharing with me my love and suffering.


I love freedom, and my love for true
Freedom grew with my growing knowledge
Of the people's surrender to slavery
And oppression and tyranny, and of
Their submission to the horrible idols
Erected by the past ages and polished
By the parched lips of the slaves.


But I love those slaves with my love
For freedom, for they blindly kissed
The jaws of ferocious beasts in calm
And blissful unawareness, feeling not
The venom of the smiling vipers, and
Unknowingly digging their graves with
Their own fingers.

My love for freedom is my greatest love,
For I have found it to be a lovely
Maiden, frailed by aloneness and
Withered by solitude until she became
As a spectre wandering in the midst
Of the dwellings unrecognized and
Unwelcome, and stopping by the waysides
And calling to the wayfarers who did
Not offer heed.

During this score and five years I have
Loved happiness as all men love happiness.
I was in constant search of her but did
Not find her in man's pathway; nor did
I observe the imprints of her footsteps
Upon the sand before man's palaces;
Neither did I hear the echo of her voice
From the windows of man's temples.

I sought happiness in my solitude, and
As I drew close to her I heard my soul
Whisper into my heart, saying, "The
Happiness you seek is a virgin, born

296

And reared in the depths of each heart,
And she emerges not from her birthplace."
And when I opened my heart to find her,
I discovered in its domain only her
Mirror and her cradle and her raiment,
And happiness was not there.

I love mankind and I love equally all
Three human kinds . . . the one who
Blasphemes life, the one who blesses
It, and the one who meditates upon it.
I love the first for his misery and
The second for his generosity and the
Third for his perception and peace.

\*    \*    \*    \*    \*

Thus, with love, did five and twenty
Years race into nothingness, and thus
Swiftly sped the days and the nights,
Falling from the roadway of my life
And fluttering away like the drying
Leaves of the trees before the winds of
Autumn.

Today I stopped on my road, like the
Weary traveler who has not reached his
Destination but seeks to ascertain his
Position. I look in every direction, but
Cannot find trace of any part of my past
At which I might point and say, "This is
Mine!"

Nor can I reap harvest from the seasons
Of my years, for my bins boast only
These parchments upon which the black
Ink is traced, and these paintings,
Upon which appear simple lines and colours.

With these papers and pictures I have
Succeeded only in shrouding and burying
My love and my thoughts and my dreams,
Even as the sower buries the seeds in
The heart of the earth.

But when the sower sows the seeds in
The heart of the earth he returns home
At eventide, hoping and waiting for

298

The day of harvest; but I have sown
The inner seeds of my heart in despair,
And hoping and waiting are in vain.

And now, since I have made my five and
Twenty journeys about the sun, I look
Upon the past from behind a deep veil
Of sighs and sorrows, and the silent
Future enlightens itself to me only
Through the sad lamp of the past.

I stare at the universe through the
Transom of my hut and behold the faces
Of men, and hear their voices rise into
Space and hear their footsteps falling
Into the stones; and I perceive the
Revelations of their spirits and the
Vibrations of their desires and the
Throbbings of their hearts.

And I see the children, running and
Laughing and playing and crying; and
I observe the youths walking with their

Heads lifted upward as if reading and
Singing the Kaseeda of youth between
The margins of their eyes, lined with
The radiant rays of the sun.

And I behold the maidens, who are walking
Gracefully and swaying like tender
Branches, and smiling like flowers, and
Gazing upon the youths from behind the
Quivering eyes of love.

And I see the aged walking slowly with
Bent backs, leaning upon their walking
Staffs, staring at the earth as though
Seeking there a treasure lost in youth.

I observe these images and phantoms
Moving and crawling in the paths and
Roadways of the city.

Then I look beyond the city and meditate
Upon the wilderness and its revered
Beauty and its speaking silence; its

Knolls and valleys and lofty trees; its
Fragrant flowers and brisk brooks and
Singing birds.

Then I look beyond the wilderness and
Contemplate the sea with all the magical
Wonders and secrets of its depths, and
The foaming and raging waves of its
Surface. The depths are calm.

Then I gaze beyond the ocean and see the
Infinite sky with its glittering stars;
And its suns and moons and planets; its
Gigantic forces and its myriad elements
That comply unerringly with a great
Law possessing neither a beginning nor
An ending.

Upon these things I ponder from between
My walls, forgetting my twenty five
Years and all the years which preceded
Them and all the centuries to come.

*   *   *   *   *

At this moment my own existence and
All of my environs seem as the weak
Sigh of a small child trembling in the
Deep and eternal emptiness of a supreme
And boundless space.

But this insignificant entity . . .
This self which is myself, and whose
Motion and clamour I hear constantly,
Is now lifting strengthening wings
Toward the spacious firmament,
Extending hands in all directions,
Swaying and shivering upon this day
Which brought me into life, and life
Into me.

And then a tremendous voice arises
From the Holy of Holies within me,
Saying, "Peace be with you, Life!
Peace be with you, Awakening!
Peace be with you, Revelation!

"Peace be with you, oh Day, who
Engulfs the darkness of the earth
With thy brilliant light!

"Peace be with you, oh Night,
Through whose darkness the lights
Of heaven sparkle!

"Peace be with you, Seasons of the
Year!
Peace be with you, Spring, who
Restores the earth to youth!
Peace be with you, Summer, who
Heralds the glory of the sun!
Peace be with you, Autumn, who
Gives with joy the fruits of
Labour and the harvest of toil!
Peace be with you, Winter, whose
Rage and tempest restore to
Nature her sleeping strength!

"Peace be with you, Years, who
Reveal what the years concealed!

Peace be with you, Ages, who
Build what the ages destroyed!
Peace be with you, Time, who leads
Us to the fullness of death!
Peace be with you, Heart, who
Throbs in peace while submerged
In tears!
Peace be with you, Lips, who
Utter joyous words of salaam while
Tasting the gall and the vinegar
Of life!
Peace bit with you, Soul, who
Directs the rudder of life and
Death while hidden from us
Behind the curtain of the sun!"

# Contemplations in Sadness

# Contemplations in Sadness

The sufferings of the multitudes are as the agonies of gnawing pain, and in the mouth of society there are many decayed and ailing teeth. But society declines the careful and patient remedy, satisfying itself with polishing the exteriors and stuffing them with resplendent, glittering gold that blinds the eyes to the decay beyond. But the patient cannot blind himself to the continuing pain.

Many are the social dentists who endeavour to administer to the evils of the world, offering fillings of beauty, and many are the sufferers who yield to the will of the reformers and thereby increase their own suffering, draw deeper of their waning strength, and deceive themselves more surely into the abyss of death.

The decayed teeth of Syria are found in her

307

schools, wherein today's youth is taught to be to-morrow's sorrow; and in her courts of justice, wherein the judges twist and play with the law as a tiger plays with its prey; and in the palaces, wherein falsehood and hypocrisy prevail; and in the huts of the poor, wherein fear, ignorance, and cowardice abide.

The political dentists of soft fingers pour honey into the ears of the people, shouting that they are filling the crevices of the nation's weakness. Their song is made to sound higher than the sound of the grinding millstone, but in truth it is no nobler than the croaking of the frogs in the stagnant marsh.

Many are the thinkers and idealists in this world of emptiness . . . and how faint are their dreams!

\* \* \* \* \* \*

Beauty belongs to youth, but the youth for whom this earth was made is naught but a dream whose sweetness is enslaved to a blindness that renders its awareness too late. Will ever the day come when the wise will band together the sweet dreams of youth and the joy of knowledge? Each is but naught when in solitary existence. Will ever the day come when Nature will be the teacher of man, and Humanity his book of devotions, and Life his daily school?

Youth's purpose of joy—capable in its ecstasy and mild in its responsibility—cannot seek fulfillment until knowledge heralds the dawn of that day.

Many are the men who curse with venom the dead days of their youth; many are the women who execrate their wasted years with the fury of the lioness who has lost her cubs; and many are the youths and maidens who are using their hearts only to sheath the daggers of the bitter memories of the future, wounding themselves through ignorance with the sharp and poisoned arrows of seclusion from happiness.

Old age is the snow of the earth; it must, through light and truth, give warmth to the seeds of youth below, protecting them and fulfilling their purpose until Nisan comes and completes the growing pure life of youth with new awakening.

We are walking too slowly toward the awakening of our spiritual elevation, and only that plane, as endless as the firmament, is the understanding of the beauty of existence through our affection and love for that beauty.

\*　\*　\*　\*　\*　\*

Fate carried me by the painful current of modern, narrow civilization, taking me from between the arms of Nature in her cool green arbour, and placing me roughly under the feet of the throngs, where I fell as suffering prey to the tortures of the city.

No punishment more severe has befallen a child of God; no exile so bitter has become the lot of one who loves one blade of the earth's grass with a fervency that causes every fibre of his being to tremble; no confinement imposed upon a criminal has approached in closeness the misery of my imprisonment, for the narrow walls of my cell are bruising my heart.

310

We may be wealthier than the villagers in gold, but they are infinitely richer in fullness of true existence. We sow in plenty, but reap naught; they reap the glorious bounty awarded by Nature to the diligent children of God. We calculate every barter with slyness; they take Nature's products with honesty and peace. We sleep fitfully, seeing spectres of the morrow; they sleep as a child upon its mother's bosom, knowing that Nature will never refuse her accustomed yield.

We are the slaves of gain; they are the masters of contentment. We drink bitterness and despair and fear and weariness from the cup of life; they drink the purest nectar of God's blessings.

Oh, Giver of Graces, hidden from me behind these edifices of the throngs which are naught but idols and images . . . hear the anguished cries of my imprisoned soul! Hear the agonies of my bursting heart! Have mercy and return Your straying child to the mountainside, which is Thy edifice!

# The Cortège

# The Cortège

The motive of Gibran in writing this work probably finds its basis in his never-ending efforts to analyze human society, its laws, rules and customs. In society Gibran perceives a general falsehood of living that leads the people from the truth, elating some persons, humiliating others. He admonishes that no individual can experience the fullness of life and enjoy the bounty of Nature while his fellowman is pursuing greed in order to attain his goal.

To illustrate his precepts, Gibran chooses two metaphorical characters. The first is *Age,* represented by a bent old man who lives in the city and suffers through its man-made laws, traditions, inheritances and corruptions. He wearies of the stifling clamor, and departs for the field in order to relax his trembling hands and meditate. In the field he meets *Youth,* symbolized by a handsome, robust young man whose eyes have seen only the trees, mountains and brooks, whose body has inhaled only the pure air, and whose ears have listened only to the singing of the streams and birds, and the whistling of the wind through the autumn leaves.

At this meeting, *Youth* is carrying a flute in his hand, preparing to greet Nature with his eternal melody of the open field. *Youth* and *Age* discuss freely their respective conceptions of life, *Age* commenting that naught but evil and misery are created in the city by human society, while *Youth* insists that only by leading a life close to the heart of Nature can one's heart find true pleasure and contentment, filling the heart's domain to its fullest with simple, God-given joy.

From this debate between *Age* and *Youth,* Kahlil Gibran's approaches to life, death, and religion are revealed. He does not propose that all persons abandon urbanity for life on the mountainside, but he endeavors to focus attention upon a simple formula for better life, and urges the people to unchain themselves from the rattling shackles of society and avail themselves, to as great a degree as possible, of the natural freedom and tranquility of rural existence. The field which Gibran describes is symbolic of the life of rich wholesomeness accruing to the heart of the person who abides close by the earth.

By reason of the nebulous, untranslatable character of the Arabic language, this play-poem is variously called *The Procession* and *The Caval-cade*. In considering Gibran's sadness as reflected herein, the translator determined that *The Cortège* was best suited, as a title, to the author's intention. This same indefiniteness, inherent in the Arabic, required occasional departure from strict translation in order that Gibran's mighty message be captured intact.

\* \* \* \* \* \*

*Age:* True, good deed by man is ever done,
  But when man is gone, evil does not

Perish with him. Like turning wheels
We are controlled by the hands of
Time where e'er man resides. Say not
"This man is famed and learned, or
Master of knowledge from the angels
Sent," for in the city the best of
Man is but one of a flock, led by
The shepherd in strong voice. And he
Who follows not the command must soon
Stand before his killers.

*Youth:* There is no shepherd over man in
The beautiful field, nor sheep to
Graze nor hearts to bleed. Winter
Departs with her garment and Spring
Must come, but only by God's great
Command. Your people are born as
Slaves, and by your tyrants their
Souls are torn. Where e'er goes the
Leader, so go they, and woe unto
Him who would refuse!
Give me the flute and let me sing,
And through my soul let music ring;

The song of the flute is more sublime
Than all glory of kings in all of time.

*Age:* Life amid the throngs is but brief
And drug-laden slumber, mixed with
Mad dreams and spectres and fears.
The secret of the heart is encased
In sorrow, and only in sorrow is
Found our joy, while happiness serves
But to conceal the deep mystery of life,
And if sorrow I were to abandon for
The calm of the field, naught but
Emptiness would be my lot.

*Youth:* The joy of one is the sorrow of the
Other, and there is no sorrow in the
Beautiful field, or sadness brought
By scornful deed. The frolicsome
Breeze brings joy to sad hearts, and
Your sorrow of heart is but a dream of
Fancy, passing swiftly, like the quick
Brook. Your sorrow would in the field
Vanish, as the autumn leaf is sped off

319

On the forehead of the brook, and your
Heart would be calm, as the broad lake
Is calm under the great lights of God.
Give me the flute and let me sing,
And through my soul let music ring;
Heaven's melody alone will ever remain,
All of earth's objects are but vain.

*Age:* Few are those content with life and far
From care. The river of the field is
But a carrier of emptiness; the river
Of human life has been diverted into old
Cups of knowledge and presented to man
Who drinks of life's richness but heeds
Not its warnings. He is joyous when the
Cups are of happiness, but he grumbles
When he prays to God and asks for the
Wealth he scarce merits. And when he
Attains his goal of iron riches his
Dreams of fear enslave him forever.
This world is but a wine shop whose
Owner is Time, and the drunkards
Demand much for little offering.

320

*Youth:* There is no wine in the beautiful
        Field, for glorious intoxication of
        The soul is the reward of all who
        Seek it in the bosom of Nature. The
        Cloud which shelters the moon must
        Be pierced with ardour if one needs
        Behold the moon's light. The people
        Of the city abuse the wine of Time,
        For they think upon it as a temple,
        And they drink of it with ease and
        With unthinking, and they flee,
        Scurrying into old age with deep
        But unknowing sorrow.
        Give me the flute and let me sing,
        And through my soul let music ring;
        The song of God must ever stay,
        All other things must pass away.

*Age:* Religion to man is like your field,
        For it is planted with hope and
        Tilled by the faithful; or it is
        Tended by the shivering ignorant,
        Fearing the fire of hell; or it is

Sowed by the strong in wealth of
Empty gold who look upon religion
As a kind of barter, ever seeking
Profit in earthly reward. But
Their hearts are lost despite
Their throbbing, and the product
Of their spiritual farming is but
The unwanted weed of the valley.

*Youth:* There is no religion in the Godly
    And beautiful field, nor any heretic
    Nor color nor creed, for when the
    Nightingale sings, all is beauty and
    Joy and religion, and the spirit is
    Soothed and the reward is peace.
    Give me the flute and let me sing,
    Prayer is my music, love is my string;
    The moaning flute will surely sound
    The misery of those in the city bound.

*Age:* What of justice and earthly rule
    That makes us laugh and weep? For the
    Criminal who is weak and poor the

Narrow cell or death awaits; but
Honour and glory await the rich who
Conceal their crimes behind their
Gold and silver and inherited glory.

*Youth:* All is justice in Nature's field; to
None does Nature grant neglect or
Favor. The trees are grown in each
Other's way, but when the breeze is
Scampering all will sway. Justice in
The field is like the snow, for it
Blankets all things, and when the sun
Appears, all things must emerge in
Strength and in beauty and in fragrance.
Give me the flute and let me sing
For the song of God is everything;
The truth of the flute will e'er remain,
While crimes and men are but disdain.

*Age:* The people of the city are enmeshed
In the web of the tyrant who rages
In fury when he grows old. In the
Lion's den there is a scent, and be

The lion there or not, the fox will
Not approach. The starling is timid
When he soars the infinite, but the
Eagle is proud, even when he dies.
The strength of the spirit alone is
The power of powers, and must in time
Crumble to powder all things opposing
It. Do not condemn, but pity the
Faithless and their weakness and their
Ignorance and their nothingness.

*Youth:* The field sees not the weak nor the
Strong, for to Nature, all are one
And all are strong. When the lion
Roars, the field does not say, "He is
A terrible beast . . . let us flee!" Man's
Shadow passes in speed through his
Brief and sorrowful visit to earth,
And rests in the vast firmament of
Thought, which is heaven's field; and
Like leaves of autumn that fall to the
Heart of earth, all must again appear in
The great springtime of colourful youth,

Beautiful in their re-birth. And the leaf
Of the tree will thrive in hearty life
After man's objects of substance perish
Into vapour and forgottenness.
Give me the flute and let me sing,
For strength of soul my song will bring;
The heavenly flute will long be cherished
But man and his greed will soon be perished.

*Age:* Man is weak by his own hand, for he
Has refashioned God's law into his own
Confining manner of life, chaining
Himself with the coarse irons of the
Rules of society which he desired; and
He is steadfast in refusing to be aware
Of the great tragedy he has cast upon
Himself and his children and their sons.
Man has erected on this earth a prison
Of quarrels from which he cannot now
Escape, and misery is his voluntary lot.

*Youth:* To Nature all are alive and all are
Free. The earthly glory of man is an

325

Empty dream, vanishing with the bubbles
In the rocky stream. When the almond
Tree spreads her blossoms on the small
Plants growing below, she does not say,
"How rich am I! How poor are they!"
Give me the flute and let me sing,
And through my soul let music ring;
The melody of God will never wane,
While all on earth is naught but vain.

*Age:* The kindness of the people is but an
      Empty shell containing no gem or
      Precious pearl. With two hearts do
      People live; a small one of deep
      Softness, the other of steel. And
      Kindness is too often a shield,
      And generosity too often a sword.

*Youth:* The field has but one great heart;
      The willow lives by the oak, and
      Has no fear of its strength or
      Its size. And the peacock's garb
      Is magnificent to behold, but the

Peacock knows not whether it be a
Thing of beauty or of ugliness.
Give me the flute and let me sing,
And through my soul let music ring;
For music is the hymn of the meek,
Mightier than the strong and the weak.

*Age:* The people of the city feign great
Wisdom and knowledge, but their
Fancy remains false forever, for
They are but experts of imitation.
It gives them pride to calculate
That a barter will bring no loss
Or gain. The idiot imagines himself
A king and no power can alter his
Great thoughts and dreams. The
Proud fool mistakes his mirror for
The sky, and his shadow for a
Moon that gleams high from the
Heavens.

*Youth:* No clever or handsome inhabit
The field, for Nature is not in

Need of beauty or sweetness. The
Running stream is sweet nectar,
And as it broadens and stills,
It reflects only the truth of
Its neighbours and self.
Give me the flute and let me sing,
And through my soul let music ring;
The moaning flute is more divine
Than the golden cup of deep, red wine.

*Age:* The kind of love for which man
    Struggles and dies is like the
    Bush that bears no fruit. Only
    The wholesome love, like the
    Enormous sorrow of soul, will
    Enliven and lift the heart into
    Understanding. When abused, it
    Is the purveyor of misery and the
    Omen of danger and the dark cloud
    Of blackness. If humanity were to
    Lead love's cavalcade to a bed of
    Faithless motive, then love there
    Would decline to abide. Love is a

Beautiful bird, begging capture,
But refusing injury.

*Youth:* The field fights not to acquire
The throne of love, for love and
Beauty abide forever and in peace
And in bounty in the field. Love,
When sought out, is an ailment
Between the flesh and the bone,
And only when youth has passed
Does the pain bring rich and
Sorrowful knowledge.
Give me the flute and let me sing,
And through my soul let music ring;
For song is the arm of love
Descending in beauty from God above.

*Age:* The youth who is visited by a great
Love through the truth of the light
Of heaven, and in whom thirst and
Hunger rage to protect that love,
Is the true child of God. And yet
The people say, "He is insane! He

Profits not from love, and the one
He loves is far from beauty, and
His pain and woe avail him naught!"
Pity those ignorants! Their spirits
Were dead before they were born on
Labour's bed!

*Youth:* No sentry or blamer abides in the
   Field, and no secret is withheld
   By Nature. The gazelle capers in
   Merriment at eventide and the
   Eagle never utters smile or frown,
   But all things in the field are
   Heard and known and seen.
   Give me the flute and let me sing,
   And through my soul let music ring;
   For music is the heart's great bliss,
   From heaven a joy, from God a kiss.

*Age:* We forget the greatness of the
   Invader but remember e'er his rage
   And madness. From the heart of
   Alexander lust grew strong, and

330

Through the soul of Kais ignorance
Was defeated. The triumph of
Alexander was naught but defeat;
The torture of Kais was triumph
And glory. Through the spirit,
Not the body, love must be shown,
As it is to enliven, not to deaden,
That the wine is pressed.

*Youth:* The memories of the lover hover
    In the field, but the deeds of
    A tyrant ne'er bring a thought,
    For his crime is recorded in
    History's book. For love, all of
    Existence is an eternal shrine.
    Give me the flute and let me sing,
    And through my soul let music ring;
    Forget the cruelty of the strong,
    To Nature alone all things belong;
    The lillies were made as cups for dew
    Not for blood or potions new.

*Age:* Happiness on earth is but a fleet,
  Passing ghost, which man craves
  At any cost in gold or time. And
  When the phantom becomes the
  Reality, man soon wearies of it.
  The river runs like the racing
  Stallion, swirling on the plain,
  Turning it to dust. Man endeavours
  That his body provide the things
  Prohibited; and when gotten, the
  Desire then subsides. When you
  Behold a man turning aside from
  Things forbidden that bring
  Abysmal crime to self, look
  Upon him with eyes of love, for
  He is a preserver of God in him.

*Youth:* Empty and barren of hope and care
  Is the beautiful field; it gives
  No heed to desire, and craves not
  For part of any thing, for God
  Almighty has provided her with all.
  Give me the flute and let me sing,

And through my soul let music ring;
Singing is love and hope and desire,
The moaning flute is the light and fire.


*Age:* The purpose of the spirit in the
        Heart is concealed, and by outer
        Appearance cannot be judged. One
        Often says, "When the soul has
        Reached perfection, then from
        Life it is released, for if the
        Soul were fruit, then when ripe
        It would fall from the tree by
        The strength of God's wind." And
        Another adds, "When the body rests
        In death the soul will depart it,
        As the shadow on the lake vanishes
        As the searing heat dries its bed."
        But the spirit is not born to
        Perish, but ever will thrive and
        Flourish. For even as the north
        Wind blows and folds the flower
        To earth, so comes the south wind
        To restore its beauty.

*Youth:* The field distinguishes not the
      Body from the soul. The sea and
      The fog and the dew and the mist
      Are all but one, whether clouded
      Or clear.
      Give me the flute and let me sing,
      And through my soul let music ring;
      For song is all of body and soul,
      From the rich depth of the golden bowl.

*Age:* The body is the womb for the
      Soul's tranquility, and there it
      Rests until light is born. The
      Soul is an embryo in the body of
      Man, and the day of death is the
      Day of awakening, for it is the
      Great era of labour and the rich
      Hour of creation. But cruelty's
      Barrenness accompanies man, and
      Intrudes upon the fertility of
      The soul's mind. How many flowers
      Possess no fragrance from the day
      Of their birth! How many clouds

Gather in the sky, barren of rain,
Dropping no pearls!

*Youth:* No soul is barren in the good
    Field, and intruders cannot
    Invade our peace. The seed which
    The ripe date contains in its
    Heart is the secret of the palm
    Tree from the beginning of all
    Creation.
    Give me the flute and let me sing,
    And through my soul let music ring;
    For music is a heart that grows
    With love, and like the spring it flows.

*Age:* Death is an ending to the son of
    The earth, but to the soul it is
    The start, the triumph of life.
    He who embraces the dawn of truth
    With his inner eyes will ever be
    Ecstatic, like the murmuring brook,
    But he who slumbers through the
    Light of heaven's day must perish

In the eternal darkness he loves.
If to earth one clings when awake,
And if he caresses Nature who is
Close to God, then this child of
God will cross the valley of death
As though crossing but a narrow
Stream.

*Youth:* There is no death in the good
Field, or graves for burial or
Prayers to read. When Nisan
Departs, the joy continues to
Live, for death removes but the
Touch, and not the awareness of
All good. And he who has lived
One spring or more possesses the
Spiritual life of one who has
Lived a score of springs.
Give me the flute and let me sing,
And through my soul let music ring;
For music opens the secret of life,
Bringing peace, abolishing strife.

336

*Age:* The field has much, man has but
  Little. Man is the spirit of his
  Creator on earth, and all of the
  Field is made for man, but man by
  His own choice flees from the nearby
  Love and Beauty of God which is the
  Beautiful field.

*Youth:* Give me the flute and let me sing;
  Forget what we said about everything.
  Talk is but dust, speckling the
  Ether and losing itself in the vast
  Firmament. What have you done that
  Is good? Why do you not adopt the
  Field as your heavenly shelter? Why
  Do you not desert the palace of the
  Noisome city and climb the knolls and
  Pursue the stream, and breathe of the
  Fragrance, and revel with the sun?
  Why do you not drink dawn's wine from
  Her great cup of wisdom, and ponder
  The clusters of fine fruit of the
  Vine, hanging like golden chandeliers?

Why do you not fashion a blanket of
The endless sky, and a bed of the
Flowers from which to view the land
Of God? Why do you not renounce the
Future and forget the past? Have you
No desire to live as you were born
To live?

\* \* \* \* \* \*

Banish your misery and leave all
Things of substance, for society
Is of naught but clamour and woe
And strife. She is but the web of
The spider, the tunnel of the mole.
Nature will greet you as one of
Her own, and all that is good will
Exist for you. The child of the
Field is the child of God.

*Age:* To abide in the field is my hope
And my longing and my desire, and
For such life of beauty and peace
I beg. But the iron will of fate

338

Has placed me in the lap of the
City, and man possesses a destiny
Which impels his thoughts and
Actions and words, and that not
Sufficing, directs his footsteps to
A place of unwilling abode.

**END**